HOPE'S JOURNEY

OTHER BOOKS BY JEAN RAE BAXTER

The White Oneida
Ronsdale Press, 2014

Respectable Appearance
Marenga Publishers (Tel Aviv), 2013

Freedom Bound
Ronsdale Press, 2012

Broken Trail
Ronsdale Press, 2011

Scattered Light
Seraphim Editions, 2011

Looking for Cardenio
Seraphim Editions, 2008

The Way Lies North
Ronsdale Press, 2007

A Twist of Malice
Seraphim Editions, 2005

Hope's
Journey

Jean Rae Baxter

RONSDALE PRESS

HOPE'S JOURNEY
Copyright © 2015 Jean Rae Baxter

RONSDALE PRESS
3350 West 21st Avenue, Vancouver, B.C., Canada V6S 1G7
www.ronsdalepress.com

Typesetting: Julie Cochrane, in Minion 12 pt on 16
Cover Art & Design: Nancy de Brouwer, Massive Graphic Design
Map: Veronica Hatch and Julie Cochrane
Paper: Ancient Forest Friendly "Silva" (FSC)—100% post-consumer waste,
    totally chlorine-free and acid-free

Ronsdale Press wishes to thank the following for their support of its
publishing program: the Canada Council for the Arts, the Government of
Canada through the Canada Book Fund, the British Columbia Arts Council
and the Province of British Columbia through the British Columbia Book
Publishing Tax Credit program.

Library and Archives Canada Cataloguing in Publication
Baxter, Jean Rae, 1932–, author
   Hope's journey / Jean Rae Baxter.

(Forging a nation)
Issued in print and electronic formats.
ISBN 978-1-55380-446-8 (print)
ISBN 978-1-55380-447-5 (ebook) / ISBN 978-1-55380-448-2 (pdf)

   1. United Empire loyalists — Juvenile fiction. I. Title.

PS8603.A935H66 2015   jC813'.6   C2015-902985-6   C2015-902986-4

At Ronsdale Press we are committed to protecting the environment. To this
end we are working with Canopy (formerly Markets Initiative) and printers
to phase out our use of paper produced from ancient forests. This book is one
step towards that goal.

Printed in Canada by Marquis Printing, Quebec

for Gill and Harry Cleghorn

Hope's Journey
(PROVINCE OF UPPER CANADA 1791)

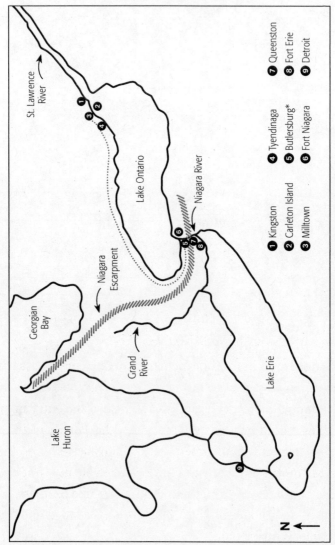

1 Kingston
2 Carleton Island
3 Milltown
4 Tyendinaga
5 Butlersburg*
6 Fort Niagara
7 Queenston
8 Fort Erie
9 Detroit

St. Lawrence River

Lake Ontario

Niagara River

Niagara Escarpment

Georgian Bay

Grand River

Lake Huron

Lake Erie

N ←

* Butlersburg renamed Newark (1792), then Niagara-on-the-Lake (1797)

CHAPTER 1

April, 1791

"I AM NOT AN ORPHAN."

Hope stood in front of the desk where Henry McIsaac sat writing in a ledger. On his desk were a stack of documents, an ink pot and a tray of quills. He finished the entry he was making, laid down his quill and raised his periwigged head. "To all intents and purposes, that's what you are."

"My mother is dead, but I have a father. He may not know I exist, but he's still my father. And I have three brothers." She felt her lower lip trembling. "A girl who has a father and three brothers is no orphan."

"Much good they do you now." Mr. McIsaac's voice was cold. "You don't seem to realize I'm trying to help you. You're lucky to be offered this position. All that Ephraim Block expects you to do is take care of his mother, keep the cabin clean and cook the meals."

As if that were nothing!

Mr. McIsaac picked up a document from the stack and placed it facing her on the desk. "According to the terms of your indentures, you'll be bound for three years. In return for the performance of your duties, you will receive food, lodging and wages of three pounds per year, payable at the completion of the three years. By that time, your father may come to claim you. Or you'll be old enough to marry."

He handed her his pen. "Make your mark above the line at the bottom of the page."

"I can write." Leaning over the desk, she carefully printed each letter. H-O-P-E C-O-B-M-A-N. Mr. McIsaac had already written the date: 15 April, 1791.

He turned the paper around and looked at it critically, causing her to wonder whether she had made a mistake. Then he signed his name as witness to her signature.

Behind her she heard a knock on the door.

Mr. McIsaac looked up. "Come in."

The door opened.

"Ah! Mr. Block." Mr. McIsaac stood up. "You're just in time."

Hope watched as Mr. McIsaac walked around from behind his desk to shake the hand of the man who had just entered.

So this was Ephraim Block. He was a thin man with stooped shoulders. His reddish hair was tied back in a queue, and his skin was coarsened by the sun.

He flicked a glance at Hope. "Is everything ready?"

"As soon as you've signed here." Mr. McIsaac showed him the paper.

"Is everything correct?"

"Of course. You know that I practised law in New Jersey for twenty years before the Revolution."

When the document had been signed and sealed, Mr. Block turned to Hope. "I suppose you have a trunk you need to bring."

Hope did not answer.

"What?" said Mr. Block. "Are you mute?" He turned to Mr. McIsaac. "You haven't saddled me with a deaf-mute, have you?"

"Not her!" He laughed. "Matron at the Orphan Asylum says she never stops talking."

"That's good. My mother will benefit from some female society, though women talk nothing but nonsense most of the time."

"Matron told me I'd be leaving today," Hope said stiffly. "I have my bundle here."

"Then let's be off," said Mr. Block. "My property is eight miles west of Kingston. I can't leave my mother alone any longer than necessary."

Hope picked up from the floor a canvas-wrapped bundle

secured by a leather strap. It held a hooded cloak that had been her mother's, two handkerchiefs, a brush and a comb. These were her only possessions.

At the door, Mr. Block turned around and said to Mr. McIsaac, "By the way, have you any news about my case?"

"Not yet. If anything comes up, I'll let you know."

"I'll be in to see you next month, as usual."

Hope followed Mr. Block out the door. She did not want to leave Kingston, where there was bustle and excitement, with bateaux coming and going up and down the St. Lawrence River, and soldiers from the Tête du Pont barracks, handsome in their red coats. Most important of all, it would be easier for her father and brothers to find her if she lived in town, not in a log cabin in the wilderness. Because she was already half a year beyond the usual leaving age, the orphanage could keep her no longer. But why was there no family in Kingston wanting to employ a servant girl?

Her bundle over her shoulder, she trudged at Mr. Block's side past the ruins of old Fort Frontenac with its crumbling walls. A stiff breeze blew from the lake.

"There's no road," said Mr. Block. "We travel by canoe. With the wind rising, the water will be rough. I'll need you to paddle in the bow."

"Paddle?" She looked at him blankly, as if she had never heard that word before. "I don't know how to paddle."

"Weren't you raised on Carleton Island?"

"I was. In the Fort Haldimand barracks. Soldiers' families were quartered there."

"I can't believe you grew up on an island but don't know how to paddle a canoe."

"Why would I? There was nowhere to go."

"Carleton Island's no bigger than three square miles, and you never left it?" He sounded as if he could not believe his ears.

Hope felt her cheeks grow red. "The only time I've ever been in a boat was when the garrison soldiers brought Ma and me over to the mainland in a bateau."

"Humph!" He said nothing more until they reached the landing. It was swarming with people, for a bateau had just arrived from Montreal. The dark-eyed *Canadiens*, wearing their bright sashes, were unloading boxes and barrels onto the shore. They laughed as they worked, shouting to one another in French. Now there would be a night of revelry at the tavern before their bateau started back down the St. Lawrence in the morning.

Mr. Block did his best to ignore the *Canadiens*. He found his canoe among half a dozen that were pulled up on the limestone shore. He shoved the bow into the water.

"Get in."

She hung back.

"Hurry up. We have to get going."

"I can't swim."

"Can't swim, either! Oh, never mind. It's not as if we are going to cross the Atlantic. Just climb in and make your way to the bow." He took her bundle from her and placed it in the canoe.

Knowing she had no choice, Hope climbed in at the stern, scrambled hand-over-hand to the bow, knelt cautiously and gripped the sides.

He reached a paddle to her. "You can't paddle if you're hanging on to the gunwales. The best way to learn something is to do it." He climbed in at the stern and shoved off.

She dipped her paddle. Hope had seen plenty of Indians paddling canoes. She had some idea of how it was done.

"Deeper!" Mr. Block called out. As she dug in with her paddle, she felt the canoe move forward. "Use your shoulders!" he bellowed.

The canoe stayed close to the shoreline as they left Kingston behind. At first the water was not too rough. But the further they went, the bigger the waves grew. One moment the canoe was borne so high on a crest it seemed ready to take flight. The next, it slapped into a trough. Half the time, Hope's paddle flailed the empty air.

It felt like the longest eight miles in the world. Her shoulders hurt and her arms felt ready to fall off. It was hard to keep a grip.

"We're nearly there," Mr. Block called to her. The next instant a big wave hit the canoe broadside.

"We're tipping over!" she screamed. But they did not. Mr. Block righted the canoe. After that, Hope clamped her jaws shut. Never again would she let on that she was afraid. She dug her paddle more deeply into the billowing water.

As they passed a clearing in the woods, Mr. Block shouted. "See that cabin? Ours is the next one."

Hope looked shoreward. Outside a log cabin, a boy was splitting logs. He lowered his axe, looked straight at her, and then lifted one arm in a big, sweeping wave.

His wave warmed her like a ray of sunshine. If she had not needed both hands to grip the paddle, she would have waved back. For the first time in days she felt like smiling. Her spirits lifted at the thought that someone young and friendly would be living not too far away.

The clearing was followed by a stretch of woods, and then they came to another clearing. Mr. Block turned the canoe landward. "We're here," he shouted, and he brought the canoe to shore.

A log cabin stood a little back from the shore, far enough back for the garden in front, which appeared to be already dug for spring planting. Behind the cabin was a plowed field in which tree stumps were still rooted. The house had a stone chimney, a plank door with long black hinges and two windows, one on each side of the door.

So this was the place where she would spend the next three years keeping house, cooking meals and taking care of Mrs. Block. Why did she need someone to take care of her? This was the part that worried Hope the most.

She lifted her bundle from the bottom of the canoe. On wobbly legs she followed Mr. Block to the cabin. He pressed the latch and opened the door. Hope heard a woman's voice.

"You're late, Ephraim." Although cracked with age, it was a voice that expected to be obeyed.

Mr. Block stepped inside. "Sorry, Mother. It was a slow

trip back. The lake was rough."

"You should have started sooner. Did you bring the girl?"

Hope felt a shiver of fear. Did that powerful voice belong to the woman who would be giving her orders for the next three years?

"Yes, Mother." Mr. Block looked at Hope over his shoulder. "Come in."

CHAPTER 2

The Tyrant on her Throne

THE OLD WOMAN SAT in a bentwood chair. She was small and shrivelled, her face deeply lined. A white ruffled cap covered her hair. The back of her chair curved around to end with an armrest on each side, and her crooked fingers clutched the armrests like claws.

Mrs. Block gave Hope a sharp look. Hope knew what she saw: a slim girl of average height wearing a grey orphanage gown that hung limply from her shoulders and reached nearly to her ankles, showing one inch of black stocking above her buckled shoes. "What's your name?" Mrs. Block asked.

"Hope Cobman."

"You're just a child."

"I'm thirteen and a half."

"You don't look it."

"She's the best I could get." Mr. Block's voice, which had sounded quite normal before, was weak and hesitant compared to his mother's.

"Let's hope she works out better than the last one."

So there had been another! Hope wondered what had happened to the last servant. The old woman probably had worked her to death.

"If it's all right with you, Mother, I'll go find the cow. It's milking time."

"You should've left Bossy in the shed, not free to wander off in the woods."

"Then she couldn't have grazed."

"If a bear got her, it will be no one's fault but yours."

When he had left the cabin, Mrs. Block turned her attention to Hope. "Did my son explain your duties?"

"He didn't tell me anything." Hope drew a deep breath. "But the lawyer in Kingston said I'd have to cook meals, clean the cabin and take care of you."

"Take care of me." Raising one hand from the arm of her chair, Mrs. Block inspected her gnarled fingers. Her hand shook as she held it in front of her face. "It's true. I can't feed myself. Can't wash myself. Can't dress myself. That's what you'll have to do for me. They should have sent a woman, not a child." Her hand dropped down to grip the armrest again.

Hope did not answer, half hoping to be dismissed as unfit for the tasks involved. But if she lost this position, what could she do? Return to Kingston? Much as she wished she could remain in town, she had no desire to live on the street among drunken sailors, cutpurses and women who had to sell their bodies to buy food to stay alive. Although the life of an indentured servant was little better than the life of a slave, it was preferable to homelessness.

"The last girl ran off with a soldier," said Mrs. Block. "When his regiment was disbanded, the government granted him one hundred acres. As soon as he had the scrip in his hand, he sold it for a pittance and went off to Montreal, taking Barbara with him. She was a good-looking girl."

Mrs. Block took a sharp look at Hope. "Your ears are too big. Jug ears. You may grow into them, but with that snub of a nose, you'll never be a beauty." She pronounced this judgment in her loud voice. "At least I won't have to worry about *you* running off with a man."

Hope felt her face turning red. "I have no desire to run off with a man."

"What is it you do desire?"

"Beg your pardon?" No one had ever before asked Hope such a question.

"Everyone has desires." She pointed to a built-in bunk that ran along one side wall from the front of the cabin to the back. "Sit down. It makes me nervous to see you stand there

shuffling from foot to foot." Hope sat down. "Well," Mrs.
Block insisted, "what do you want most, if it isn't a handsome man to carry you away?"

Hope knew exactly what she wanted most, and she saw no
reason to make a secret of it.

"I want to find my father and my brothers. I have three
older brothers."

"Oh! Where are these missing people?"

"I don't know."

"When did you last see them?"

Hope hesitated. "The only one I've ever seen is my middle
brother, Elijah. He was a private in a Loyalist regiment, the
King's Royal Rangers of New York. For a while he was stationed at Fort Haldimand on Carleton Island. That's when I
saw him. But then the army sent him down south."

"Why have you never seen your father or your other
brothers?"

"My father and Silas, my oldest brother, were away fighting the rebels when I was born. Ma said my father never
knew about me. He joined Butler's Rangers before she realized she had a baby on the way."

"So your father and two of your brothers fought for King
George against George Washington. That's something you
can be proud of. What about your youngest brother?"

"His name was Moses. Oneida Indians carried him off. I
was told they adopted him. That's all I know. Ma said he was
a constant thwart and torment to her. But I'd like to find him,
just the same."

"How old was he when they captured him?"

"Not quite ten."

"He likely was a thwart and torment. Boys that age usually are. But he's a grown man now. If you find your brothers, they'll be more like uncles to a child like you."

"That would be fine. I like the idea of having uncles to look out for me."

"Nonsense. A woman should take pride in looking out for herself." She cleared her throat. "I'd like a cup of tea. The water bucket's inside the door. You know how to make tea, don't you?"

"Of course." Hope thought she could figure it out.

The tea canister stood on a shelf supported by long pegs driven into cracks between the logs. The shelf also held a teapot, several tin cups and bowls and an earthenware mixing bowl.

Next to the shelf was the fireplace. It was equipped with a spit for roasting meat and a swing-out crane with two hooks, from one of which hung a large pot. A low fire burned. Steam rose from the copper kettle that rested on the hob.

Hope felt Mrs. Block's eyes upon her as she lifted the kettle from the hob, poured hot water into the teapot and added a handful of tea leaves.

"Stupid girl!" said Mrs. Block. "Just as I expected."

Hope flushed. "I'm not stupid."

"What's that? Impertinent, too? I don't tolerate backtalk from anyone. Now pour that mess into the slop bucket under the shelf, rinse the pot with boiling water, then put in the tea leaves. Add the water last."

After following these directions, Hope sat down on the bunk and looked around while the tea steeped. The cabin was constructed of notched logs laid one upon the other to a height of about seven feet. The logs of the front and back walls were fully twenty feet long. Gaps between the logs were filled with clay. There was a puncheon floor of split logs laid upon the earth, flat side up. A partition that extended from the back wall halfway to the front wall created a semi-separate space that held a bed covered by a patchwork quilt. Under this bed nestled a small trundle bed.

Having completed her inspection, Hope asked, "Do you think the tea is ready?"

"It should be. Pour me a cup. You'll have to help me hold it."

When Hope had poured the tea, she placed the cup in Mrs. Block's hand, and then cupped her own hand around the old woman's bony fingers. Together they raised the cup to Mrs. Block's lips. When she nodded, Hope concluded that the tea was satisfactory.

Mrs. Block had finished her tea when her son came in carrying a pail of milk.

"Have you ever drunk fresh milk straight from the cow?" he asked Hope.

"No, sir."

"Try it. Tomorrow the cow goes to the Andersons. Enjoy the benefit while you can."

She took a cup from the shelf and scooped up enough milk to fill it.

"Thank you, Mr. Block."

"Call him Ephraim," snapped his mother. "My late husband was Mr. Block. We don't want any confusion."

Hope didn't see what confusion there could be, since the original Mr. Block was no longer of this world.

A pained expression crossed the younger Mr. Block's—Ephraim's—face. Hope had the feeling that he did not enjoy his demotion. He continued speaking as if he had not heard. "That cow is the reason we're still alive. Three years ago, in 1788—they call that the Hungry Year—Bossy's milk was the only thing that kept us from starvation."

"We Loyalists came here with nothing," Mrs. Block said bitterly. "Because we opposed the Revolution, our own neighbours turned against us and drove us from our homes. And how did Britain reward us for our loyalty? She gave us a tract of wilderness to clear, a few tools and half a cow."

Hope raised her head. "What do you mean, 'half a cow?'"

Ephraim explained, "My mother means one cow for every two families. Britain also supplied the Loyalist refugees with rations for three years. After that, we were expected to raise our own food." He gave a humourless laugh. "As if three years were long enough to clear the forest, dig out the rocks, plow fields and start producing crops. Yes, we owe our lives to Bossy."

As Hope listened, she sipped the milk. "It's very good." She licked her lips to catch every drop.

"Enjoy it while you can," said Ephraim. "Tomorrow the

cow goes to the Andersons. It's their turn to have her. The Andersons' land is next to ours."

"Is that where I saw a boy splitting logs?"

"Yes. Adam. He's the oldest. They have eleven children."

"Twelve," his mother corrected him.

"What's one more or less?" He shrugged. "We've a road half made to connect their place and ours. You can drive the cow there tomorrow. They keep the cow for five days and then bring her back to us for two days. We've worked out this arrangement because the Andersons have many more mouths to feed than we do."

"I don't know how to drive a cow," said Hope.

Mrs. Block snorted. "It doesn't sound as if you know how to do anything."

Ephraim came to Hope's rescue. "Don't worry. Bossy knows the way. You just have to flick her rear end with a switch to keep her moving."

They supped on pork and beans. As Hope spooned food into the old woman's mouth, she began to feel sorry for her. It must be terrible to be as helpless as a baby.

"I hope you're a tolerable cook," Mrs. Block said at the end of the meal. "Pork and beans is the only thing Ephraim does well."

Ephraim looked sheepish. "My split-pea soup isn't so bad."

"If you ignore the lumps."

"I can't cook at all," said Hope, wanting to make Ephraim feel better.

"Then I'll have to teach you. Any simpleton can learn to make soup without lumps."

Hope wondered why Ephraim didn't follow Barbara's example. He must sometimes have been tempted to run away.

When evening came, Hope helped Mrs. Block get ready for bed. As she undid the many buttons of her gown, tugged it off over her head and struggled to get her into her nightgown, she wondered how poor Ephraim had coped with all these preparations.

After Mrs. Block was settled under her quilt, Hope pulled out the trundle bed. She took off her own gown and, having no nightgown, lay down in her undergarments.

She folded her arms under her head, stared up at the darkness and contemplated her situation. This had been a most eventful day. She had survived her first journey by canoe and her first taste of taking care of Mrs. Block. Although the old lady was a tyrant, Ephraim seemed pleasant. Tomorrow she would meet the friendly boy who had waved to her. Life was not so bad. Hope closed her eyes and was soon sound asleep.

CHAPTER 3

Woeful

EPHRAIM LED BOSSY FROM the lean-to shed that was built onto the cabin's back wall. She was a brown cow with large, vacant eyes. "She's a good cow," said Ephraim, "but even for a cow, she's not very bright. Every few steps you have to give her a switch on the rump to remind her to keep moving." He gave Bossy's rear end a flick with a slender willow wand to show how it was done. The cow took three steps forward.

"Now you try it." He handed the switch to Hope. She gave a delicate flick. The cow walked two yards before she stopped. Hope gave another flick. It worked.

"Just keep at it," Ephraim advised. "Let her know that you're the one in charge."

The half-made road was easy to follow. Ephraim and his neighbour had cut down trees and removed brush to make a corridor twenty feet wide. They still had to dig out the stumps and level the ground. When that work was completed, they would have a road that would accommodate a wagon and a team of oxen. At present, Hope and the cow had to wend their way amongst the stumps.

With frequent applications of the switch to keep her moving, Bossy led the way. It was a sunny spring day. Although the trees had not yet budded into leaf, a carpet of trilliums covered the forest floor. A robin sang cheerfully.

Before long, Hope and Bossy emerged from the woods onto the open space where the cabin stood. There was the boy, splitting logs again. As soon as he noticed Hope, he lowered the axe, resting the axe head on the ground. Hope raised her hand to shade her eyes from the glare of the morning sun. From under her palm she inspected the boy's face. It wore an amused expression, lips twisted in a half-smile. He had hair the colour of straw, a big, sunburnt nose and green eyes. He did not move but simply waited for her to approach. Neither said anything until he was at the cow's head, and she was at the other end.

"Adam?" she asked.

"That's me. I know who you are. You're the girl in the canoe."

"Hope Cobman. I've come to work for the Blocks."

"I wondered who they'd get this time." He looked her up and down, from her limp mobcap to the scuffed toes of her shoes. "You look like an orphan. Are you an orphan?"

She stiffened. She had been prepared to like him, but now she wasn't sure. "How does that matter to you?"

"Hey! I've nothing against orphans. In fact, I wish I were an orphan."

"Really? Why?"

"I'm fourteen years old. If I were an orphan, I'd be on my own. I could go wherever I liked. But I'm not an orphan, so I'm stuck here splitting wood."

"Where would you like to be?"

"Montreal."

"What's so good about Montreal?"

"There are crowds of people and something different to do every day. Folks live in real houses, with iron stoves to heat them."

"What's a stove?"

"It's a new American invention . . . Say, don't you know anything? I'll wager you've never been to school."

Her silence must have made him feel guilty. After a moment he said, "I'm sorry. I didn't mean to be rude. It's not your fault if you haven't been to school."

His lips twisted in the half-smile she had noticed before. Since he looked as if he expected her to accept his apology and return his smile, that was exactly what she refused to do.

"You aren't angry at me, are you?" He looked suddenly dejected.

"Of course I am." As soon as she said it, she realized that she no longer was.

Just then a dog joined them, sidling up to Adam with an apologetic manner. Burrs were sticking in its ragged coat. One eye was missing, as well as half an ear. It was a female, black and white, thin, with bulging flanks.

Hope exclaimed at her appearance. "That dog looks terrible!"

"Woeful always looks terrible."

"What kind of dog is she?"

"Welsh sheepdog. I don't know why we keep her. We don't have any sheep."

Woeful looked up, head cocked, wagging her tail.

"When she's in heat," Adam continued, "we lock her in the shed. She usually manages to dig her way out. One time a bear must have mauled her. She always comes back pregnant. We have to drown the puppies."

"That's so cruel!"

"What else can we do? Most of her litters are half wolf. We'd let her keep one pup to comfort her if we thought we could find it a home."

"Poor puppies! Poor Woeful!" Then the words spilled out without Hope even thinking. "I wish I had a puppy."

He laughed. "Be careful what you wish for." He bent down and scratched behind the dog's torn ear. "We don't drown her puppies in front of her. Woeful doesn't know what happens to them. Six months later, she whelps again."

He straightened up. "Come and meet my mother. She's almost as fertile as Woeful, but we keep Ma's pups."

Hope gasped. What a sassy boy! She had never before met anyone like him.

"Mrs. Block says there are twelve of you."

"That's right. Three boys and nine girls. I was born first. Next came two girls, but they both died before they were a year old. Then Ma had the twins—both boys. After that, it's been one baby girl after another for nine years. Pa's fed up. He needs boys to build this farm."

"Where are your brothers and sisters? I don't see them anywhere about."

"The ones old enough to hold a knife are out back with Pa, girdling trees. The little ones are in the cabin."

Hope and Adam left Bossy munching green shoots that poked out of the soil. As they neared the cabin, the wails of a crying baby told Hope that all was not well within.

When Adam opened the door, the first thing Hope noticed was a squalling baby lying in a cradle that looked as if it had been carved from a tree trunk. A girl about four years old was rocking the cradle. Two more girls, little more than infants themselves, were rolling around on the floor, shrieking and pulling each other's hair. When they saw that they had a visitor, they stopped fighting, sat up and stared at Hope.

Sitting on a stool was a woman mending a shirt. She looked up when Hope and Adam came in. She was a thin woman with pale skin. She wore a mobcap that was too big for her face, making her small features look pinched and her large grey eyes enormous. Something about the woman's face made Hope think of a wounded animal.

She could hardly imagine how crowded the cabin must be

with the whole family—fourteen people—in it at the same time.

"Mama," said Adam, "this is Hope Cobman from the Blocks' place. She's brought us the cow."

Mrs. Anderson laid down her needle and looked closely at Hope. "They're lucky to have found somebody to help them. Ephraim's been afraid of losing his land."

"Lose his land? How could that happen?"

"He has two hundred acres. To get full title, he has to build a house, clear one acre each year and make a road to connect to the nearest neighbour on each side. If he doesn't, the government will cancel his location ticket. But how can he do everything required while waiting on that old woman hand and foot?"

Mrs. Anderson took another stitch, sewing up a broken seam. "Truth to tell, I don't know why Ephraim bothers. He has no children. It's not as if he had anybody to inherit a farm after he dies."

"He still might marry and have a family," Hope suggested. "He's not old."

"Ephraim's forty. But he can't marry. He has a wife."

"A wife? Where is she?"

"She left him."

Hope now felt thoroughly confused. "Is that Barbara?"

"No. Barbara was a servant. His wife's name is Philippa. Philippa from Philadelphia. A fine young lady. She ran off with an English officer. They went to England."

The baby was still bawling. Mrs. Anderson rose from her stool, picked her up and patted her back. The baby belched loudly. The crying stopped.

"That's my good girl," said Mrs. Anderson, putting the baby back in the cradle.

"I must go," said Hope. "Mrs. Block needs me."

When they were outside, Hope said to Adam, "Do you suppose Mrs. Block drove both of them away, the servant and the wife?"

"I suppose so. Ma's sure that's the reason."

This did not sound good.

CHAPTER 4

What's in a Name?

DURING THE NEXT FOUR DAYS Hope learned how to make split-pea soup without lumps, cook rabbit stew and mould beeswax candles.

On the morning of her fifth day she was outdoors emptying a pan of dishwater when she saw Adam approaching with the cow. Bossy came to a halt at the corner of the cabin. Her tail moved a little, swishing slightly.

Adam's big red nose was peeling. *He ought to wear a hat,* she thought, *to keep off the sun.*

"I can't stay long," he told her. "Pa and I are building a fence to keep animals out of our vegetable garden. He said one of the twins could bring the cow. But I told him I had something to tell you. I have a question to ask you, too."

"First, what do you want to tell me?"

"Woeful whelped yesterday. Six puppies. Two looked like wolf cubs, and three like nothing in particular. But one looks pure sheep dog. Male. Black and white. That's the one I saved for you."

Hope didn't know what to say. She had told Adam that she wished she had a puppy, but she was sure she hadn't actually *asked* for one. What if she wasn't allowed to keep it?

He frowned. "You don't look happy. I hope you still want a puppy. If you won't take it, I'll have to drown it."

Hope shuddered at the thought. "Of course I want it. How long before it's old enough to leave its mother?"

"Eight weeks."

"Fine." Eight weeks gave plenty of time to convince Ephraim and Mrs. Block that they needed a dog. "Now, what's the question you want to ask?"

"It's about you, if you don't mind. When I asked if you were an orphan, you didn't give a straight answer. So I wondered."

"I don't mind telling you. The truth is, I'm not an orphan. My mother died last year, but my father is alive . . . so far as I know. He was a sergeant in Butler's Rangers."

"How did you lose touch with him?"

"We never were in touch. He doesn't know I exist. But I hope he'll find me someday."

"That doesn't make sense. He's not going to look for you if he doesn't know you exist."

"It isn't me he'd be searching for. He'd be trying to find my mother. The problem is, he wouldn't know where to look. We lived in Canajoharie in the Mohawk Valley. My father had already gone off to war when rebels burned down our house. My mother fled with some other Loyalist families to the British fort on Carleton Island. Nobody in Canajoharie knows that. If he went there to ask about her, no one could tell him where she went. But since he fought for King George, he couldn't go back to Canajoharie anyway."

Adam nodded. "So if you want to find your father, it's up to you to start looking."

"I don't know how."

"It shouldn't be difficult. Even you could do it. All the Loyalist regiments have been disbanded. My father is sure to know where Colonel Butler settled his Rangers. Do you want me to ask?"

She narrowed her eyes at the slight. Even *I* could do it! She felt like telling him not to bother. But since she really did want to know, Hope gritted her teeth and said, "Yes. Please ask."

"Glad to. When you bring back the cow, I'll tell you what I've found out."

The empty dishpan in her hands, Hope watched Adam until he disappeared around a turn in the half-made road. She didn't know whether she liked him or not, finally deciding that she did, but not as much as he liked himself.

Bossy stood placidly chewing her cud. A shout from Mrs. Block broke the silence. "Hope, what are you doing out there? You haven't brushed my hair."

"Coming!" Hope hurried into the cabin.

All that day she kept thinking about her father. Ma had described him countless times. Although Hope had never seen a picture of him, she carried a clear image in her mind. He had brown eyes, dark hair and bushy black eyebrows. He was tall and thin. There was about him a strong odour of pipe tobacco.

He had always seemed like a storybook figure, vivid but not quite real. For all her dreaming about him, she had no more expected him to enter her life than she expected Jack the Giant Killer to come knocking at the door. Now, as finding her father began to seem possible, she felt suspended somewhere between reality and a dream. Only one thing was certain: if she did find him, she would never feel alone again.

That night she dreamed about him. He was standing beside a doorway looking down at her. It was the doorway of a house she knew of but had never seen. He seemed on the point of holding out his arms to embrace her, but he did not move. His eyes were brown, his eyebrows black and bushy. His expression was tender and loving. She caught a whiff of pipe tobacco. He did not speak. Hope had the feeling that if she waited a little longer, he might.

Two days later, Hope urged the cow as fast as she could along the way to the Andersons' place. Bossy's clanking cowbell announced their arrival. Adam and his father, who were digging post holes, put down their spades.

If she hadn't known who Mr. Anderson was, she could have guessed in an instant. Adam's father was an older, taller, heavier version of Adam. Father and son had the same green eyes and big nose. Mr. Anderson's nose was not peeling; he had the sense to wear a hat with a wide brim.

After introductions, Mr. Anderson said, "Adam tells me you're trying to find your father."

"And my brother Silas. They both served in Butler's Rangers."

"This is what I can tell you. When Butler's Rangers were disbanded, Colonel Butler secured land to settle his men on the west bank of the Niagara River. That was six years ago. Butler is now commanding officer of the Nassau Militia. If you want to ask about your father and brother, try writing to Colonel John Butler. Nassau Militia, Butlersburg, West Niagara."

"Thank you, sir. I'll ... I'll ... do that." Write a letter! It would be just as easy to flap her arms and fly like a crow to Niagara.

"Now," said Mr. Anderson, "Adam has something to show you."

"Your puppy," Adam explained with a grin.

She followed him into a lean-to shed built onto the back of his family's cabin. There on a bed of straw lay Woeful, with her lone puppy attached to a teat. Woeful opened her one eye, raised her ragged ear and gave a thump of her tail. The puppy looked perfect. He had tiny bent legs and already the beginnings of a black and white coat like his dam's.

"Woeful looks so happy," said Hope. "I wish you hadn't given her that dreadful name."

"It suits her. Why, just look at her! I've never known a more woeful dog. One eye. Half an ear. Full of fleas."

"A name should be more inspiring. My name is Hope."

"I know that."

"But you don't know that I was born two months earlier than I should have been. My mother gave birth to me in the woods, after rebels burned our house. It was November, and very cold. Everybody thought I was going to die, but they didn't name me Hopeless."

"You're not a dog. Woeful doesn't know what it means." He bent over and scratched behind her half-ear. "What are you going to call your puppy?"

"I shall name him Captain, because that will encourage him to be brave." She knelt in the straw and with a fingertip stroked the puppy's back. He was so tiny that he could have fitted into the palm of her hand.

Woeful sighed and closed her eye.

Hope rose. "I need to hurry back. I don't know what I'll do about that letter to Colonel Butler. To write such a letter is beyond my skill. Ma taught me my ABC's, but little more. I'll need help." She looked at him. "Do you think maybe you could . . . ?"

"I don't think so."

"You've been to school."

"Two years at Mrs. Canahan's Sylvan Seminary for the

Young Ideal. I wanted to go to the Schyler School in Milltown, but my father thought Mr. Schyler had dangerous ideas about democracy. Mrs. Canahan had no ideas at all, so she was safe. After a couple of years, Pa took me out of school because he needed me here. I wasn't learning much anyway." Adam hesitated. "You need an educated person to help you with your letter, not somebody like me."

"Whom would you ask if you had an important letter to write?"

Adam scratched his head. "That's a good question. I might go to Milltown and ask Mr. Schyler. People say he's amiable."

"Is he the same Mr. Schyler that Charlotte Hooper married? His first name was Nick."

"Mr. Schyler's first name is Nicholas; I suppose he's the same person. I don't know anything about his wife."

"It *must* be Charlotte Hooper! I heard that her husband became a schoolmaster." In an instant, Hope's plan took shape in her mind. Of course Charlotte would help her. Hope's mother had given Charlotte and her parents a safe place to hide during their flight from the Mohawk Valley. Charlotte had known Hope since the day she was born. Their families had shared danger and hardship. And now Charlotte was married to a schoolmaster.

Hope turned to Adam. "How far away is Milltown?"

"An hour's walk through the woods. Half that by canoe."

"So close! I know what I'm going to do. I'll ask Mrs. Block to give me half-a-day off. I can walk to Milltown and tell

Charlotte about the letter. She will ask Nick to help me, and of course he will." Hope was almost bouncing with excitement. "Thank you, Adam. You've been a great help."

It was all so simple! She felt like singing as she walked back to the Blocks' cabin, thinking that to someone with a name like Hope, anything was possible.

CHAPTER 5

Hatching a Plan

A MONTH PASSED AND nothing came of Hope's plan to seek Charlotte's help with the letter. Hope waited for the right moment to ask for half-a-day off, but the right moment never came. She cooked and cleaned and took care of Mrs. Block. Although Hope did her best, the old woman was never satisfied.

Trees came into leaf. Black flies bit. The warming air was filled with birdsong and mosquito hum. Bossy plodded back and forth, providing milk for each household in turn. Every time Hope took the cow to the Andersons' place or Adam brought her back, he wanted to know what she had done about the letter.

Her answer was always the same. "I have to wait for Mrs. Block to have a good day. If she's having a bad day, there's no point asking permission to go to Milltown. She'd just bite my head off."

Finally he lost patience with her. "You're Hopeless!" he said, making a wry face.

"What do you mean by that?"

"I mean, that should be your name."

Hope winced. "You don't know what Mrs. Block is like."

"She isn't a fire-breathing dragon."

"That's what you think."

Adam scratched a mosquito bite on his neck. "Do you want to find your father, or not? Because if you do, you have to show some spunk."

All that day she thought about what he had said. It was cruel of him to call her Hopeless. But was he right? A person could spend a lifetime waiting for just the right moment, and it might never come. It was time for her to take a chance.

That evening after supper Hope was darning a stocking by candlelight. Ephraim was sprawled on the bunk, tired after scything hay all day.

Mrs. Block's loud voice broke the silence. "Ephraim, we must buy some chickens."

Hope raised her head, startled.

"Chickens?" Ephraim sounded surprised.

"You heard me. Hope doesn't have enough work to keep her busy. She can take care of them."

Is she serious? Hope waited to learn more.

"Where would we keep chickens?" Ephraim asked.

"In the shed, where Bossy stays when she's here. That's just two nights a week. It's a waste to let the shed stand empty the rest of the time. You can put up some nesting boxes. There'll still be enough room for the cow."

"Hmm." Ephraim said drowsily. "Fresh eggs. Chicken stew."

Hope turned her attention to the stocking. As she ran the yarn around the hole, she imagined a flock of happy hens clucking and scratching and bobbing about. She liked the idea even if it meant more work.

Ephraim sat up. "Mother, if you're serious, there's a poultry dealer who's brought in breeding stock from across the border. He'd sell us a few pullets and a young rooster. Now that I have the haying done, I can see him tomorrow. He lives in Milltown."

"Milltown!" Hope gave such a jump that she stabbed her thumb with the darning needle. "Ephraim, may I come, too?" The words tumbled out of her mouth.

His eyebrows rose. "There's not much to see in Milltown. It's not like Kingston."

"The very idea!" exclaimed Mrs. Block. "Your place is here."

Hope seized her chance. "Mrs. Block, do you remember what you said to me the day I came here?"

"I expect I said a number of things."

"There was one thing in particular. You said, 'What is it that you want most?' And I said, 'I want to find my father and my brothers.'"

"What does this have to do with Milltown? Surely you don't expect to find them there!"

Hope expelled a deep breath. "Adam's father says that Colonel Butler settled his Rangers near Niagara. My brother Silas and my father served in that regiment. If I write a letter to Colonel Butler, he can tell me where I'll find them."

"So you want to write a letter. I still don't see what this has to do with Milltown."

"I'll need help to compose it," said Hope. "Mr. Schyler the schoolmaster is married to someone who's known me since the day I was born. If I ask her to ask him, maybe he'll help me write to Colonel Butler."

"So you want to leave me here alone while you traipse off to Milltown."

"It won't take long."

"Young woman, you don't seem to understand your position in this household. You are an indentured servant." Mrs. Block's voice grew louder and louder. "You are our property. The whole of you. Every minute of you. Don't you dare forget it."

Her needle poised over her work, Hope could scarcely believe what she was hearing. As the words sank in, she felt rage boiling up inside. She jumped to her feet, darning egg, yarn and stocking tumbling onto the floor. She doubled her fists. "I am not your property. Even if you're the Devil's grandmother, you don't own my soul!"

Mrs. Block's face turned purple. "How dare you speak to me like that! Impudent, useless, stupid girl."

"Mother," Ephraim said gently, "don't let yourself become upset. Dr. Sills warned you."

"That quack!"

Hope picked up the darning egg and stocking and sat down. She didn't care what happened now. Whatever the outcome, she did not regret one word of what she had said. She began to weave the yarn back and forth across the hole.

Ephraim rose from the bunk, crossed the room to where the water bucket stood on the floor, lifted the dipper from its peg on the wall and scooped up a dipperful. After taking a long, deliberate drink, he said, "Mother, I'll need help with those chickens. Can't you spare Hope for a couple of hours? She can speak to the schoolmaster's wife while I'm doing business with the poultry dealer."

"Are you taking that girl's side against me?"

"No, no! Just stating a fact."

"Of course I can manage on my own for a few hours. But I don't want this to set a precedent, as Mr. McIsaac would call it. I've had servants before. Remember Barbara? Give them an inch and they'll take an ell."

"Hope understands her position in this household." He gave Hope what she thought was a sympathetic glance, and then he added, "Just as I understand mine."

Hope lowered her face to hide her smile. The stocking she was mending belonged to Ephraim. The hole was in the heel. She wove the yarn back and forth carefully so that the mend would be smooth and flat, without a lump to vex his foot.

CHAPTER 6

Milltown

IN THE MORNING HOPE was on her best behaviour. She was cheerful and patient as she dressed Mrs. Block, brushed her hair and spooned porridge into her mouth. Ephraim, too, seemed to be trying hard to please. After Hope had settled Mrs. Block in her chair, he made sure the pillow at his mother's back was in exactly the right spot, and he tucked a blanket around her legs. Mrs. Block appeared determined not to appreciate the extra effort being made.

"We'll be back at midday with the chickens," Ephraim said as he and Hope were about to leave. "Don't worry. Hope will have plenty of time to do her work when we return."

Mrs. Block turned her face away and refused to look at either of them. She ignored her son's conciliatory goodbye.

While they were launching the canoe, neither Hope nor Ephraim made any reference to the tense situation. Hope climbed in at the bow and picked up her paddle.

"Beautiful day," she said, by way of conversation.

"Indeed, it is. June is my favourite month."

She plunged her paddle into the rippling water. As the sunshine warmed her back, her fear of an upset vanished like the mist over the calm water.

They reached Milltown in mid-morning. It was a small town built on a creek that emptied into Lake Ontario twelve miles west of Kingston. A short way upstream, a mill's gigantic wheel turned slowly in the millrace. The shoreline consisted of broad limestone ledges, like a flight of steps that marched down into the water. When Ephraim had steered the canoe to shore, Hope climbed out onto a ledge, holding up the skirt of her gown so that no drop of water would touch it.

After Ephraim had pulled the canoe onto the shore, he turned to her. "The school is on the main street, so you'll have no problem finding it. The schoolmaster's house is next door."

"Where will you go to buy the chickens?"

"The poultry dealer lives on the outskirts. It's not far. I'll meet you here. If I'm back before you, I'll wait."

"Don't you need my help to carry the chickens to the canoe?"

He shrugged. "I can manage."

"You told your mother that you needed me to . . ." She did not finish the sentence, for suddenly she realized that his words to his mother had been merely an excuse. His reason for bringing her to Milltown was to help her, not the other way around. She hesitated. "Well, then . . . thank you . . ."

"Good luck," he said, but he did not move.

She waited, wondering what else he had to say.

"I don't know whether I ought to speak of this," he said, "but it's been on my mind ever since I realized who you are. My mother told me about your father and your brothers."

"If you have something to tell me, please do."

Ephraim took a deep breath and let it out. "It's about Elijah"

"What about him?"

"I knew him slightly. We both served in the King's Royal Regiment of New York, the Royal Greens. I remember when he joined. He was just a boy of thirteen, and as keen as they come. When he developed into a first-rate marksman, he was chosen for a Loyalist unit that Major Patrick Ferguson was training to fight against General Washington's forces in the South. After joining Ferguson's unit, Elijah was sent to the Carolinas and I never saw him again." Ephraim paused. "But I heard about him."

"You mean that you know he deserted."

"Yes." Ephraim hesitated. "I've been waiting for a chance to tell you how sorry I am. When a man loses a limb, you know how he's been hurt. But there are wounds to the mind that the eye cannot see. Somebody in Elijah's position—he's a casualty, not a coward." Ephraim cleared his throat. "That's all I wanted to say. You and I both have business to do. No time to waste talking. I'll see you here when you're done." He took a coin from his pocket. "Here's a shilling to have your letter stamped."

"Oh! Thank you! I hadn't thought about that."

After Ephraim had left her, she stood for a few moments thinking about what he had said. He seemed to be preparing her for disappointment in case she succeeded in finding Elijah. But it wasn't Elijah she was looking for right now. Her sights were set on finding her father and Silas. She had only two hours to carry out this part of her plan. Hope tucked the shilling in her pocket, smoothed the skirt of her gown, made sure that her hair was tucked neatly under her mobcap and started down the street.

She passed a blacksmith shop. The door was wide open, allowing her to see the smith at his forge hammering a piece of red-hot iron. The next place she came to had a sign over the entrance: COFFINS AND FURNITURE. Then Hope walked by a general store: HOOPER'S PROVISIONS. Through its window she saw metal pails, steel traps, iron pots, axes and bolts of cloth in many colours. An old man wearing a canvas apron was leaning on a crutch while he talked to a customer.

Next she came to a small white building with a bell mounted on the roof. There was a sign above the door:

SCHYLER SCHOOL. The door was not just closed, it was pad-locked. There were two windows at the front, one on each side of the door, and four more along the side wall. All were shut. Hope stepped up to one of the windows. Through the glass she saw four rows of double desks. The desks faced a table, behind which a blackboard was attached to the wall. There was no teacher in the schoolroom, nor were there any scholars. Dead flies lay on the windowsill.

She should have known that in June the school would be closed. Every boy would be out in the fields, hoeing or hay-ing, and every girl would be at home, learning to cook, spin and weave.

She stepped back from the window. Next to the school was a small white house with black shutters. An apple tree stood in the front yard. Her head up and her shoulders squared, Hope walked briskly along the short path that led from the school to the house. She stepped onto the low porch, her heart beating fast, and rapped on the door.

CHAPTER 7

The Letter

THE SMILING WOMAN WHO came to the door wore a slightly askew mobcap from which a strand of curly black hair had escaped. Hope recognized Charlotte at once, for she had changed little since the last time Hope had seen her. Through the open doorway Hope saw a cradle and also three children, two boys and a girl, playing with alphabet blocks on a braided rug. They looked up at Hope, their expressions friendly and curious.

Charlotte's smile faded and a frown creased her brow. She looked puzzled. Maybe she was wondering who this girl on her doorstep was and where she had seen her before.

"Good morning, Mrs. Schyler. I'm Hope Cobman."

That was all it took. "Of course you are! But you mustn't call me Mrs. Schyler. I'm Charlotte." The smile had returned, and Hope felt herself being dragged indoors. "You were just a little girl last time I saw you. When was that? Six years ago? Still, I should have recognized you." Placing her hands on Hope's shoulders, she took a steady look. "You have the eyes, the ears and the snub nose. Yes, you're a Cobman through and through."

Then Charlotte introduced her children. That was baby Joan asleep in the cradle. The little ones playing on the rug were Isaac, Martha and Jack. After Hope had told the children that she was happy to meet them, and they had replied that they were likewise happy to meet her, they went back to playing with their blocks.

"You had only one baby the last time I saw you," Hope said.

"That was Isaac. But he isn't a baby any longer. Isaac is eight years old. Martha is five and Jack is three. Joan's my only baby now. She arrived six months ago." Charlotte paused. "But you didn't come here to meet my children. What about you? I've lost track of you since Nick and I settled in Milltown."

"After the peace treaty gave Carleton Island to the United States, the Loyalists living there had to be evacuated. My mother and I were moved to Kingston." Hope hesitated. "Ma died a little over a year ago."

"I'm so sorry! I didn't know." Charlotte took Hope's hand. Although Hope tried not to cry, tears filled her eyes. "That must have been terrible for you," said Charlotte. There were tears in her eyes, too.

Hope wiped her eyes. "For a year I lived in the orphanage. But after I passed my thirteenth birthday and they could keep me no longer, I became indentured to a man named Ephraim Block to take care of his invalid mother."

"I've heard of him," said Charlotte. "Don't he and his mother live a few miles east of Milltown?"

"That's so. Ephraim brought me here to find you. I need some help, and you seem the best person to ask."

"Me?" said Charlotte. "Well, why don't you sit down? We'll have a cup of tea while you explain what I can do." She took cups, saucers and a teapot from a shelf.

Hope sat down at the table. It was a long table, and it looked new, the pine boards as white as if they had just come from the sawmill.

"I'm trying to find my father and my brother Silas," said Hope.

Charlotte lifted the kettle from the fireplace hob. "I don't see how I can help with that."

"I think you can. I need someone to help me write a very important letter. Since your husband is the schoolmaster, I thought you might ask him if he would."

"You'd better start at the beginning," said Charlotte as she made the tea. "I never met your father or Silas. They'd already gone off to war when your mother hid my parents and me in her root cellar."

When the tea was ready, she sat down across from Hope. Charlotte poured the tea, and Hope began her story. She described everything that had happened to her in the past six years, pausing only to take the occasional sip of tea. Finally, she told Charlotte about the discovery that her father and Silas were probably living at Niagara. "And so," she concluded, "I want to write to Colonel Butler, the commanding officer of the Nassau Militia at Niagara, to ask if he can tell me where my father and Silas are settled."

"That's quite a story," said Charlotte. "I'm sure Nick would want to help you, but he's a schoolmaster only from October to April. From spring planting until harvest time, my husband is a farm labourer. He won't be home until after sunset."

"Oh, dear! I can't stay that long," said Hope. "Mrs. Block can't be left alone all day."

"Then let me help you."

"Could you?"

Charlotte laughed. "I'm not a scholar like Nick, but I had seven years of schooling, and I write a fair hand. I have paper, pens and sealing wax."

Hope's spirits brightened. "I'd be so grateful!"

Charlotte rose from the table. The room had shelves on both sides of the fireplace. The shelves on one side held dishes, bowls and canisters of various kinds. Those on the other side were loaded with books as well as a tray of quills and an array of tiny boxes and pots. While Charlotte mixed ink powder from one of the boxes with water, Hope explained what she wanted to say. Then Charlotte took paper and a quill pen, sat again at the table and wrote it down.

> *Dear Colonel Butler,*
>
> *I am searching for my father Sergeant John Cobman and my brother Private Silas Cobman. They served in your regiment. If you can tell me where they are and how to reach them, you will have my sincere and undying gratitude.*
>
> *Please write to me care of Lawyer Henry McIsaac in Kingston.*
>
> *Your obedient servant,*

After Hope had signed her name, Charlotte asked, "How shall I address it?"

Remembering what Adam's father had told her, Hope said, "To Colonel John Butler, Nassau Militia, Butlersburg, West Niagara."

Hope watched, fascinated, while Charlotte folded the paper, addressed it, melted sealing wax in a spoon over a candle and poured the crimson blob to seal the letter shut.

"Milltown has a post office," said Charlotte. "If you wish, I'll take your letter to be stamped by the postmaster. Then it will go on board the next packet boat with the mail bound for Niagara. It's due here in three days. After that, all you'll have to do is wait." She paused. "That sounds easy, though I know from experience that waiting is the hardest part."

"I have a shilling to pay for the letter to be stamped," said Hope, and she took the coin from her pocket and placed it on the table.

"Thank you. I wasn't going to mention money," said Charlotte, "not after all the help your mother gave my family." She picked up the coin. "A shilling should cover the postage. I haven't sent many letters, but I know that the cost depends on distance and the number of sheets of paper."

Hope rose to her feet. "Now I must go. Ephraim may already be waiting for me at the landing place. He came to Milltown to buy chickens. He's probably had more than enough time to do that."

"Come visit me again," said Charlotte as she pulled back her chair from the table. "We have more to talk about. I can tell you things that your mother never knew." Her voice grew solemn. "Especially about Elijah."

"He's the only one of my brothers I've ever seen," said Hope. "I was four when he visited Ma and me on Carleton Island. I'm not sure whether I have a real memory of him or just something made up from things she told me."

Charlotte and Hope stood facing each other. "My earliest memory of Elijah is as clear as if I first met him yesterday," said Charlotte. "I was fifteen; he was thirteen. My parents and I were refugees from the Mohawk Valley, travelling north to Canada through the bush. Papa tripped on a tree root and sprained his ankle. He couldn't walk. We had to find a safe house for a few days while he rested. I set out for Canajoharie, which was a mile away. When I reached it, I peeped in people's windows, trying to find a place where Loyalists would be welcome."

"How could you tell that," Hope asked, "from looking in people's windows?"

"I was hoping to see a portrait of King George, or anything that would show allegiance to England. So there I was peering through a window when something hard jabbed me in the back and a voice called out, 'Halt! Or I'll drive this pitchfork through your kidneys.' That was Elijah. He marched me into the house, thinking he'd caught a spy. After I explained who I was and why my parents and I needed shelter, your mother let us stay in the root cellar. That's when my friendship with Elijah began. It's curious how often our paths crossed over the next few years. On Carleton Island. In Charleston. In a South Carolina swamp."

"Where is he now?"

Charlotte shrugged. "I don't know. Last time I saw him, he was heading for Cherokee country. Maybe that's where he's living now. He can never come back."

Hope nodded. "I know. When we were living in the barracks on Carleton Island, a mean boy taunted me. He said Elijah was a deserter and he'd be shot if they caught him. I asked Ma if this was true, and she started to cry."

"It's true." Charlotte sighed. "I talked with Elijah before he deserted. The state he was in nearly broke my heart. He'd been through more in the war than he could bear."

Baby Joan awoke with a cry. The other children, tired of their game, began to crowd around Charlotte, demanding her attention. Hope and Charlotte rose from their chairs. Charlotte gave Hope a hug and walked her to the door.

When Hope reached the street, she turned to wave. Charlotte, standing in the open doorway with the baby in her arms, called, "Let me know when you have any news."

A feeling of intense loneliness came over Hope after the door closed. On one side of that door was Charlotte with her children. On the other side was Hope, who had no one.

She straightened her shoulders as she set off down the street, back to the landing place. She had done her part. In three days her letter would be on its way to Niagara. The rest would follow. When she found her father, she would never be lonely again.

CHAPTER 8

Snowflake

WHEN HOPE RETURNED, Ephraim was sitting on a limestone ledge smoking his pipe. The bottom of Ephraim's canoe was covered with snow-white chickens lying on their backs, scaly yellow legs straight in the air. Each chicken had its hook-nailed feet lashed together with twine.

"I'm sorry if I kept you waiting," said Hope.

"I haven't been waiting long." He knocked his pipe against the rock to empty the bowl and then stood up. "The poulterer's boy helped me carry the chickens to the canoe. Did you write your letter?"

"Mrs. Schyler wrote it for me. She'll make sure it goes to Niagara on the next packet boat."

"How will Colonel Butler reach you with his answer?"

"I've asked him to write to me in care of Lawyer McIsaac in Kingston."

"Good idea. Henry McIsaac is looking after my case. I see him in Kingston once a month. If there's a letter for you, I can pick it up."

Ephraim's case? Hope figured it wasn't her business to ask what that meant. She turned her attention to the chickens. They were not struggling, but lay quietly in the bottom of the canoe, apparently resigned to whatever fate awaited them.

"Seven pullets and a rooster," said Ephraim. "The pullets aren't laying yet, but they will in a few weeks."

"They look half-dead."

"They'll be lively as soon as we get them home and free their feet."

Hope climbed into the canoe and took her place in the bow, kneeling on the only spot not covered by chickens.

From Milltown to the Blocks' land was an easy paddle. Hope and Ephraim were back at the cabin by midday. When they had reached shore and climbed out of the canoe, he lifted a hen by its feet. "Carry this bird into the shed. Set it on the floor."

Hope took the chicken from his outstretched hand and held it at arm's length in case it suddenly revived and started pecking her with its beak. The hen made a weak clucking sound. Ephraim followed her to the shed, carrying two more.

When the chickens were all in the shed and the door was closed, he severed the cords that tied their feet. Within seconds, the chickens came to life, as Ephraim had said they would. The rooster crowed. The hens clucked. All the birds rustled their feathers and stretched their wings.

All but one.

A single pullet, the smallest of the seven, lay limp on the shed's dirt floor.

"The poulterer threw that one in for half price," said Ephraim. "It won't be much of a layer. We'll have it in the stew pot before long."

Hope picked up the runt. It huddled against her chest, settling into her arms like a kitten. *Cluck cluck*, it said, nestling softly. Its feathers were white as snow, and its down was softer than rabbit fur.

"That's right," said Ephraim. "By keeping it warm you improve its chance to thrive. But don't treat it like a pet. You know the farmer's rule."

"What's that?"

"Never give a name to anything you expect to eat."

He left the shed and closed the door.

Hope pushed her face into the bird's feathers. As she felt its heart beating, a warm feeling of pure affection flowed through her.

"Your name is Snowflake. You're a runt. But that's all right. I was a runt for a long time before I started to grow. You will, too. As soon as you're old enough, you're going to lay an egg every day. Then you won't have to go into the stew pot."

Cluck cluck. The pullet snuggled in her arms.

CHAPTER 9

Mysteries of the Old Indian Trail

THREE DAYS LATER, Hope was down at the shore filling the water bucket when the packet boat appeared in the east, its sails dazzling white against the blue sky.

Her letter to Colonel Butler was on that ship. It must have made its stop to pick up passengers and mail at Milltown that very morning. How long would it take to reach Niagara? And when it got there, what would happen? The Colonel must be a very busy man. Would he find time to write to her? If he did, how long would it take for his answer to reach her?

She followed the ship with her eyes until it disappeared in the west. Then she carried the bucket back to the cabin. Her next task was to let the chickens out of the shed so that they could scratch in the dirt to pick up beetles and other tasty morsels. Snowflake, a blur of white, flew out the shed door. Although the smallest, she had become the liveliest of the flock.

Hope checked the nesting boxes. No eggs yet. She left the shed and was watching the chickens bob about when she heard Mrs. Block bellow, "Hope! What's keeping you? I want a cup of tea."

"Coming!" Hope hurried inside. As she prepared the tea, she waited for the first "Stupid girl" of the day. But Mrs. Block had something else on her mind.

"I happen to be partial to raspberries," she announced. "There must be some ripe by now."

"I noticed some raspberry bushes when I was taking Bossy back to the Andersons' yesterday," said Hope, "but there weren't many ripe berries."

"I suppose you ate all that you found?"

Hope did not answer. Of course she had eaten them! What else were raspberries for?

"There's better picking along that old Indian trail," said Mrs. Block. "When you have your work done, you can take a basket to gather any you find."

"What old Indian trail?"

"Haven't you noticed? It starts at the shore a couple of hundred feet west of our cabin and leads back north into the bush. I suppose it's overgrown by now. Three years have gone by since the last time I went berry picking."

Hope made the tea, cut up a rabbit that Ephraim had shot

and put it into the stew pot to simmer. She rounded up the chickens, who clucked their protest at being locked up again after so short a spell of freedom. As soon as she had them shut in the shed, she started out.

The beginning of the Indian trail was obscured by undergrowth, but once she had found it, the path was easy to follow. Even if no one used the trail now, nature had not yet taken it back completely.

Mrs. Block was right about the berries. More raspberry bushes grew along this trail than along the way to the Anderson place. But few berries were ripe. Hope walked half a mile before she had gathered enough to cover the bottom of her basket. She might as well give up, she thought, and return in two or three days when the berries had had more time to ripen.

Hope was just about to turn back when suddenly she heard a strange sound. DUM, *doom*, DUM, *doom* DUM. Drumming. Where was it coming from? Hope stood listening, held in its spell.

On Carleton Island she had heard Mohawk drums many times, the sound rising from the Indian camp outside the Fort Haldimand palisade. This drumming was different, though she could not have said exactly how. *Come closer*, the rhythmic throbbing seemed to say.

She smelled smoke on the air. Not ordinary wood smoke. This odour was oddly sweet, drawing and repelling her at the same time. Her skin prickled, and a chill ran down her spine.

She turned around and began to walk, slowly at first, then faster, glancing over her shoulder from time to time. She was running by the time she reached the cabin. At the door, she stopped and took a deep breath before pressing the latch.

Before Mrs. Block had a chance to ask what had kept her so long, Hope blurted, "I heard drumming back in the woods, and there was a strange smoky smell."

"Sweet grass," said Mrs. Block. "There must be Mississaugas hanging about. Indians don't understand that when you sell your land, there's an obligation to leave. If they come to the cabin, don't give them anything to eat. Otherwise, we'll never get rid of them."

"Are they dangerous?"

"No. Just a nuisance. Now get busy. Put the raspberries into a bowl and add some potatoes to the stew. Ephraim will be back for supper any time now."

The next day, Indians showed up at the cabin door. There were two men, two women and half a dozen children. One woman had a baby in a cradleboard strapped to her back.

So these were Mississaugas. They looked different from the Mohawks she had seen around Fort Haldimand. No scalp locks. The men, like the women, had their hair in braids. Their clothing was a mixture of ragged cloth and leather. They looked tired and thin.

"Go away!" Mrs. Block shouted from her chair. "We have no food to give you!"

The Indians spoke to each other in their own language. One of the women held up a broom, the other a birch-bark basket. These people weren't beggars, Hope realized. They had come to trade.

"We don't need your brooms and baskets," Mrs. Block shouted. "Go away!"

"I'm sorry," Hope said before shutting the door.

"You don't need to apologize to them," said Mrs. Block.

The Indians quietly left. As Hope watched, they reached the start of the old trail and in moments disappeared into the forest. So it was their drumming she had heard and their sweet-grass smoke she had smelled.

Two days went by, two days of sunshine for ripening more berries. Hope set out eagerly. She picked and picked until her fingers were scarlet with raspberry juice. But though she found plenty of berries, there was no trace of the Indians. She kept on walking beyond the place where she had heard the drumming. When her basket was nearly full and she was thinking it was time to turn back, she came suddenly to a small creek, its rushing water tumbling over rocks. On the creek bank stood a log cabin. She stopped and stared.

It was a small cabin, perhaps eight feet by ten. No door. A scrap of greased rawhide dangled from one corner of the empty window frame. Pegs whittled to a sharp point had been set into the head jamb of the door frame, and it looked as if something—a blanket or an animal hide—had once hung there to cover the entry.

Fascinated, although somewhat afraid, she called, "Anybody here?" No answer. She called again. Still no answer. Hope tiptoed inside. The air in the cabin had the same smoky, sweet odour that she had smelled two days ago. Mississaugas had been here. They were here no longer.

That they had moved on seemed reasonable. What puzzled her was the presence of the cabin. Why was it here? It was not one of those bark shelters that Indians made. Though small, it was built like a settler's home.

By the time Hope returned to the Blocks' cabin, the sun was losing its heat and the shadows were lengthening. Mrs. Block looked as if she couldn't decide whether to be angry that Hope had been away so long or happy that she had returned with such a feast of raspberries.

The berries won. While Hope fed them to her, Mrs. Block showed no reluctance to answer questions.

The cabin, she said, had been built by an old man who called himself the Squire. He was mad, but had a lot of sense about some things. He must have lived with the Indians at some point, because he knew what roots and berries were good to eat. He set snares for animals. He fished in the creek.

"Was he a hermit?" Hope asked.

"You could call him that. He thought he could live in that cabin for the rest of his life without being disturbed. But after the war ended, Britain bought this land from the Mississaugas. All of us entitled to a Loyalist grant put our names on a list deposited with the quartermaster general. We drew our location tickets from a hat. Ephraim drew this lot. When he took possession, he was mighty surprised to find the Squire living on his land.

"When Ephraim told him to leave, the Squire claimed that possession was nine-tenths of the law. I told Ephraim to have the sheriff throw him off. But Ephraim turned soft-hearted, telling me that even if he cleared an acre a year, he'd never clear that far back in his lifetime. So he let the old man stay."

"Nobody lives there now," said Hope.

"No. The winter before last there was a bad cold snap. Ephraim went back to check on the Squire. There he was sitting in his cabin, his back against the wall, frozen solid, with his limbs splayed out like a wooden doll's. If the Squire did have squatter's rights, they died with him."

Hope shivered, picturing what it would be like to find a dead man sitting in a cabin frozen stiff. "After that," she asked, "who used the cabin?"

"Indians, from time to time. I told Ephraim to tear it down, but he hasn't got around to it yet."

Hope was glad that Ephraim did not always follow orders. Despite the Squire's fate, she liked the idea of a cabin hidden in the woods.

CHAPTER 10

Disaster

HOPE PULLED A WARM EGG from the straw. It was the fifth she had found today, and she still had two nesting boxes to check. The chickens were all outside the shed, scratching in the dry earth.

"Hope!" Mrs. Block bellowed from inside the cabin. "What's taking you so long?" Since the shed and the cabin shared a common wall and there were gaps between the logs of that wall, Mrs. Block's rebuke sounded loud and clear.

Hope bristled. Mrs. Block had sent her to look for eggs only a few minutes ago. Now she was complaining before allowing Hope enough time to check the boxes thoroughly. A sixth egg remained to be found; Hope was sure of that. The young hens were clever at hiding their eggs. Yet no hen could suppress the urge to cluck with pride every time she laid an egg. "Look what I've done!" she seemed to say. Thus Hope knew how many eggs she could expect to find.

She uncovered the missing sixth egg, which was buried in the straw, and added it to those in the bowl she was carrying.

"Stupid girl!" Mrs. Block exclaimed as Hope entered the cabin. "Will you never learn to come when I call?"

Hope held out the bowl to let Mrs. Block see the six small white perfect eggs.

"There should be seven." Mrs. Block's tone implied that Hope was at fault.

"One of the hens hasn't started laying, but she will."

"If she hasn't yet, she'll never be any good. Now make me a cup of tea. Then you can take Bossy over to the Andersons."

After Mrs. Block had finished her tea, Hope rounded up the seven hens and the rooster and shooed them into the shed. She gave Snowflake a cuddle and then left the shed, closing the door behind her.

It was the sort of sultry summer day when the air is still and nothing stirs. Bossy, lying in a patch of clover chewing her cud, was not interested in going anywhere. Hope had to flick her regularly with the switch to keep her moving. Only the mosquitoes were active; Hope had a dozen new bites by the time she reached the Andersons' place.

Adam was waiting for her, and he was not waiting alone. The puppy was with him, sniffing around the woodpile in the yard. As Hope approached, Adam picked him up.

"You have to take him today." He thrust Captain at her. "He's ten weeks old. Woeful pushes him away. Pa doesn't want a half-wolf around the place. He would have drowned him with the rest, except I promised you'd give the pup a home. But you keep putting it off."

"I can't take him today," said Hope. "I haven't asked Mrs. Block or Ephraim if I can keep him. Please give me one more week. I have to find the right moment."

Adam shook his head. "If you don't take him now, Pa's going to put him down."

What choice did she have? Hope took the puppy. She carried him part of the way. Whenever she set him down, he ran about, investigating every hole in the ground that might house a chipmunk or other small creature. He did not seem to notice that the day was too warm for spending so much energy.

It would have been faster to pick him up and carry him all the way, but Hope was in no hurry. She needed time to think up reasons why the Blocks should have a dog. As a watch dog to warn off prowling Indians? No. That would not work; the few Indians in the area posed no danger. As a hunter to spring rabbits and grouse for Ephraim to shoot? No. That wouldn't work either. Sheepdogs were for herding, not hunting. As a guard to protect the chickens from foxes and mink? That might work . . . unless they suspected that Captain was half wolf.

Hope faltered at the cabin door. Maybe she should find

somewhere safe to leave Captain for a couple of hours . . . until she found the right moment.

The shed was the only place she could think of. She took him there. A couple of hens were walking around on the dirt floor; others were roosting in their nesting boxes. She didn't see Snowflake.

She set down Captain and pulled together a small pile of nesting straw as a bed. The puppy seemed to know what it was for. Worn out from his walk, he climbed onto the straw and lay down. With a sigh he rested his muzzle on his fore-paws and closed his eyes. The hens paid no attention.

Before leaving the shed, Hope looked around anxiously. Where was Snowflake? There was no way the little hen could have escaped from the shed. Someone must have taken her. Hope held her breath as she walked to the cabin door, opened it and stepped inside. There, on top of an upturned bucket lay Snowflake's headless body.

"You're slow getting back," said Mrs. Block. "You certainly like to take your time."

Hope choked on a sob. "Snowflake!"

"What?"

"Did Ephraim kill her?"

"If you mean that runt pullet, of course he did. It never laid an egg and never would. Now you can take it outside to pluck and draw. Put the feathers in a sack. Just the soft ones. We'll save them for a pillow. Keep the gizzard, heart and liver. They'll go into the stew for supper tonight."

"I'm not going to eat it," Hope muttered as she left the

cabin, carrying the chicken, a sack, a sharp knife and a bowl.

She sat on the doorstep, wanting to cradle Snowflake's body but unable to take her eyes from the bloodied stump where the head ought to be. After a long time she said to herself, *Snowflake's gone. This isn't Snowflake. It's just a dead bird.*

Hope began to pluck, saving the down feathers and leaving the rest to go into the midden. When the body had been stripped, she used the knife to enlarge the vent under the tail. She thrust her hand inside. Amidst the soft, wet entrails she felt something hard and smooth.

From Snowflake's body she drew out a perfect egg.

And there were more. At least a dozen. These were still soft. They ranged from one that was full size to an egg that was smaller than a thimble.

Ephraim found her weeping when he returned to the cabin at midday for something to eat. Tears running down her cheeks, she held out the bowl to show him its contents: the gizzard, heart and liver . . . and the perfect egg. She thought he would say something about the egg, but he did not.

"You made a pet of that pullet, didn't you?"

"Yes."

"Remember what I told you: never give a name to any creature you expect to eat."

"I didn't expect to eat her."

"You know that sooner or later every chicken ends up in the stew pot. You mustn't be sentimental about food animals. God created them for us to eat."

Apparently regarding the discussion as closed, Ephraim

was about to enter the cabin, when suddenly a strange commotion rose from the shed. There was clucking and squealing and yapping.

"Something's got in with those chickens!" Ephraim raced to the shed. Hope did not move. If the hens didn't kill Captain, then Ephraim would.

She waited. Any moment now, Ephraim would appear with the puppy. Dead or alive. Hope kept her head low when she heard him coming around the corner.

"Look what I found." She raised her head. He gave her a look that was more amused than angry. "This young fellow was chasing hens all around the shed. I don't suppose he has anything to do with you?"

"Maybe."

"Did he come from the Andersons' place?"

"He might have."

Ephraim sat down next to her, holding Captain carefully.

"I don't suppose you know his name?"

"Captain."

"We'll have to tell my mother."

"Does she like dogs?"

"Hates them."

"Oh."

CHAPTER 11

The World Turns Upside Down

"OVER MY DEAD BODY!" Mrs. Block bellowed. "You're not keeping a dog in this cabin." Her hands gripped the armrests of her chair, and her eyes were almost popping out of her head.

"Please, Mother, don't let yourself become excited. You know what Dr. Sills said last time."

Hope scooped up Captain in her arms and edged her way to the door. She felt for the latch. With her eyes on Mrs. Block's face, which was purple, she opened the door and slipped outside.

"Whew!" Hope held up the puppy so that they were nose to nose. Now for the first time she noticed that his eyes were yellow. He had wolf eyes. From his sire. Had Ephraim noticed it, too?

Inside the cabin, Mrs. Block was still shouting. "There. Will. Be. No. Dog."

"Now, Mother. I'll make sure that the dog is no trouble. When my case is settled, there'll be money to buy sheep. The dog can herd them. He'll be worth his keep."

"I told you if we gave Hope an inch, she'd take an ell. I've had bad servants before, but that girl is the worst of the lot. Sneaky. Deceitful."

"Mother, you know that's not true. Hope's a good girl."

"You always take her side against me. We'll get rid of the dog and the girl, too."

"What are we going to do?" Hope asked the puppy, whose eyes fastened on hers with a trusting expression, as if he were sure she would think of something. "I know," she said. "We'll stay in the shed until this blows over. But you must not worry the chickens."

She carried him into the shed and set him down. At the sight of Captain, the three hens that were walking about on the floor took flight to the safety of their nesting boxes.

Hope sat on the floor. The puppy crawled onto her lap. While she was patting him, she kept her ears tuned to what was happening on the other side of the log wall that separated the shed from the cabin. It was easy to hear everything through the gaps between the logs. Mrs. Block used words that Hope never expected to hear from a lady. The old woman was beside herself with rage.

Afterwards, Hope wished that Mrs. Block had expressed herself differently. Phrases such as, "as long as I live," and "over my dead body," did not seem well chosen. Or perhaps they were too well chosen. At any rate, Mrs. Block's outbursts ended abruptly. Hope heard a hoarse gasp, a crash and then silence. She shivered. The sudden quiet was more frightening than the shouting before.

Then she heard Ephraim's voice. "Mother? Mother? Oh, my God!"

What had happened? A stroke? A seizure? Hope cowered with the puppy on the floor while the chickens huddled in their nesting boxes. On the other side of the wall Ephraim was mumbling and moving about.

Hope did not know what to do. Should she leave the shed and go to the cabin to ask if she could help? Or would it be better to wait until Ephraim came to find her, as sooner or later he certainly would? She decided to wait.

The shed had no window, but the gaps between the logs were wide enough to let her know that the light was starting to fade. Hope was feeling hungry and was sure that Captain was hungry, too. Inside the cabin, the pot of chicken stew was simmering over the fire. Hope had put it on to cook before Ephraim told his mother about the dog. The stew smelled delicious. Of course Hope wasn't going to eat one bite of it. But it smelled delicious, anyway.

She was relieved when at last she heard Ephraim's voice. "Hope, are you in the shed? If you are, please come here. I have something terrible to tell you."

"I'm here. I'm coming." Captain followed her to the cabin.

Ephraim met Hope at the door, which he opened only half way, using his body to block her from seeing what was inside.

"My mother has gone from this world to a better place." He stepped aside to allow Hope to enter. Now she saw that he had laid Mrs. Block's body on her bed, where she lay with her hands folded upon her bosom. Her face looked more peaceful than Hope had ever seen it before.

She felt no sorrow. Maybe this meant she was a wicked, heartless girl, for she felt worse about Snowflake's death than about Mrs. Block's. But she did feel sorry for Ephraim, remembering her own grief when her mother had died.

"I'm sorry for your loss," she said gravely.

"Thank you." Ephraim breathed deeply, and then he said, "Before it's completely dark, one of us should go to tell the Andersons. There are many things that need to be done. Mother's body must be prepared for burial. A grave must be opened. Mr. and Mrs. Anderson will help us."

He began to walk back and forth very fast, his feet thumping on the split logs of the puncheon floor. "I knew this might happen. Dr. Sills warned her." He clutched his head with both hands as he paced. "Apoplexy. She had a seizure in the spring. Before you came."

Since the room was small, with the bunk that ran along one wall taking up two feet of space, pacing the floor involved many quick turns. At last he stopped. "This was bound to happen sooner or later. It's a shock, anyway."

"I'll go to tell the Andersons," said Hope, "before it's too dark. May I leave Captain with you?"

"Of course you may." He reached out to take the puppy from her arms.

Hope ate the chicken stew. An inner voice said that she should be ashamed of herself, but she was too hungry and too tired to care.

The next few days passed in a blur. Hope helped Mrs. Anderson lay out Mrs. Block's body and sew it into the blanket they used for a shroud. A bateau brought a coffin from Milltown. Adam and his father dug a grave among the trees. The Reverend Mr. Stuart came from Kingston to conduct the burial service. Mr. McIsaac was there, as well as a few others from Kingston and Milltown. All the Andersons attended, Adam looking stiff in a black coat that was too short and too tight. Women brought cooked meats and puddings.

When all the food had been eaten and the company departed, Hope and Ephraim were alone in the cabin. Captain, the innocent cause of everything, lay sleeping on a folded blanket on the floor. Hope made a pot of tea. As she poured, she thought how strange it was that Mrs. Block was not there to complain about it being too weak or too strong, too hot or too cold.

Ephraim sat in the bentwood chair. It took a few minutes for Hope to get used to seeing him in Mrs. Block's chair. He looked more relaxed than he had ever seemed in his mother's presence.

"This is very good tea," he said. "Thank you. And thank you for everything you've done. No one could have taken better care of my mother. You were always so patient."

"She had good days and bad days. It didn't take long to understand the reason. It had to do with pain."

"You're a wise girl." He held out his cup for Hope to refill. "My mother lived her last years in pain, and many years in the shadow of loss. Before that, her life was easy." A faraway look crossed his face. "Our home was in New Jersey. My father was a merchant. He dealt in fine furniture and china imported from England. I was their only child. By the time I was your age, I was already learning the business, knowing I would take it over someday. That day came sooner than expected. My father died when I was twenty. Because he had trained me well, the business continued to prosper. Mother and I had a comfortable life.

"In 1775 everything changed. Politically, we were Tories, loyal to King George. That made us unpopular with the people who wanted independence."

"That's what happened with my family too," said Hope. "Ma told me how rebel neighbours looted our house and burned it."

"Such things happened to many Loyalists. There were mobs in the streets. They broke the windows of our show-room. Mother and I talked about leaving, but all our money was tied up in the business. We thought that somehow we could last it out." Ephraim took a deep, shuddering breath. "One Sunday, as Mother was on her way home from church, a mob attacked her. They stripped her naked. A respectable woman sixty years old. Naked. That was how she walked the rest of the way home."

Hope could not even speak, imagining how mortifying that would be.

"We left that night. I wish we'd taken more time to pack, but Mother was in hysterics. There were dozens of legal papers I should have brought with me. I failed to do so."

"Were you very rich?"

"Tolerably wealthy. For the past five years I've been trying to obtain compensation for what my family lost. Mr. McIsaac is working on it."

"I've heard both you and your mother mention something called 'your case.' Is that what you meant?"

"Yes, but I won't bother you with that story. It's a comfort having you here. You must be tired. I know that I am." He stood up, stretched, and then crossed the room to lie down on the bunk.

Hope pulled out her trundle bed from under Mrs. Block's bed. Tomorrow she would take Mrs. Block's sheets down to the shore to scrub on the rocks. She considered the future of the bed. Would Ephraim take it over as well as the chair? It looked much more comfortable than the bunk in which he had been sleeping.

She was truly tired, yet she slept fitfully that night, disturbed by Ephraim's snoring—which had never bothered her before—and also by images that would not leave her mind. Her own mother's funeral. The orphanage. The things that Ephraim had just told her. Most of all, she could not stop wondering what lay in store for her now that Mrs. Block was no more.

CHAPTER 12

An Immodest Proposal

LIFE RETURNED TO NORMAL, although it was a new kind of normal. Ephraim cleared land, hoed weeds and scythed hay. Hope cooked, cleaned, looked after the chickens and led Bossy to the Andersons' homestead at the appointed times.

She trained the puppy to sit, stay and come. Then she started teaching him to herd the chickens. An eager pupil, Captain would round up the six hens and the rooster several times a day and drive them into the shed. He enjoyed this game more than the poultry did.

In the evenings Ephraim sat in Mrs. Block's bentwood chair, except that now it was Ephraim's chair. He gazed into the fire and said little. Hope, bent over her mending, wondered what was going on in his head.

In August, three weeks after the funeral, Ephraim made one of his regular visits to Kingston to learn what progress Mr. McIsaac had made in his case. There was nothing to report. Nor was there any news for Hope. Colonel Butler had still not answered her letter.

But Ephraim did bring back something for her. A cap. It was a simple white cotton mobcap like any other, but crisp and new, not limp and bedraggled like the one she had been wearing.

"A little gift to thank you for all that you do," he said.

Of course she was pleased to have her work appreciated. She liked the cap and tried it on, tucking the smooth coil of her brown hair inside.

"You're a pretty girl," he said.

No one had ever called her a pretty girl before. Big ears. Pug nose.

"Thank you." Feeling her cheeks redden, she lowered her face.

He was not finished, for suddenly he caught both her hands in his and gave them a squeeze. Startled, she looked up. He let her hands go. That was all. Nothing truly offensive was said or done. But the way Ephraim had seized her hands gave Hope an uneasy feeling that the ground had shifted under her feet. She wished that Ephraim had not bought her a new cap. She wished that he had not called her a pretty girl or squeezed her hands.

While she washed the dishes after supper that evening, he sat in his chair smoking his pipe. Every moment she felt his eyes on her. She dried the dishes, put them on the shelf and took the pan of dishwater outdoors to dump. As soon as she returned, she planted herself in front of him.

"We should talk about my indentures."

"What about them?"

"My indentures bound me to look after your mother."

"And you did a wonderful job. Please sit down. I agree that it's time to talk."

She sat on the edge of the bunk, facing him.

"Here is what I have to say." He set down his pipe. "Your life will be easier now that you are freed from that burden. There's no need to cancel your indentures. I want you to stay. Now that Mother's gone, I don't want to live like a hermit."

"Of course not." She remembered what Mrs. Block had told her about the crazy old Squire alone in his tiny cabin back in the woods. "That would be a wretched life."

For a few moments Ephraim appeared to be examining his fingernails. Then he said, "I'd marry you if I could."

Hope gasped. "Marry!"

"But I can't. There is an obstacle."

She was speechless. Just one obstacle! She could think of two without even trying. First, he already had a wife. Second, he was forty years old and she was not yet fourteen.

Without waiting for an answer, he continued. "Since I cannot marry you, I want to assure you that I shall always be as respectful, caring and loyal as if you were my lawful wedded wife. You have my solemn promise that I will make provision for whatever . . . issue . . . results from our union."

As she took in his meaning, a shiver started at the back of her neck and ran right down to the bottom of her spine. Hope felt sick all over. She stood up.

"No."

"I thought you might say that," he said calmly. "But at heart you are a practical young woman, with more sense than sensibility. When you think it over, you may change your mind."

Her lips curled with anger. "Never. Never. Never." With each repetition her voice grew louder, and she felt her skin becoming hot with rage. "What have I done to deserve this insult? Is it because I'm poor?" Her hand doubled into a fist. He did not move, but sat looking up at her, unperturbed.

"Hope," he said calmly, "this display will get you nowhere."

"Display!" She flew at him, both fists pounding his insolent face. He caught her wrists. Now he was on his feet, pushing her back onto the bunk.

"No!" she screamed.

He stood over her, gripping her wrists so hard they hurt. "This is completely unnecessary. I'm not going to force you." Then he let her go.

She rose from the bunk and went outside and sat on the step. Just before dark she re-entered the cabin, pulled out her trundle bed from under Mrs. Block's bed and dragged it across the floor toward the cabin door.

"What are you doing?" Ephraim asked.

"I'm taking my bed to the shed," she growled as she tugged it *bump, bump, bump* over the uneven puncheons.

"Don't be ridiculous."

She ignored him. When she reached the door, he opened it for her and watched silently as she dragged the bed outside.

The hens clucked their consternation as she manoeuvred the bed through the shed door. From their nesting boxes they watched her position it in the middle of the shed and lie down. Captain had remained in the cabin. She wished that she had called him to come with her, but now it was too late to do anything about that. She pulled her blanket up to her chin. "Good night," she said loudly, speaking not so much to the chickens as to the man who was listening—she was sure he must be listening—on the other side of the wall.

In the morning she emerged to make breakfast. She did not speak to Ephraim. She did not want to be in the same space with him, and so she took her food outside and ate her porridge sitting on the step while she wondered what to do next. Tonight Bossy would be back. There would not be room in the shed for both the cow and the bed.

When Ephraim finished eating, he came outside and sat down beside her. She moved as far away from him as she could.

"You don't need to act like this," he said. "I'm a gentleman. You aren't in any danger."

She refused to look at him.

"You're old enough to understand a man's need for a woman."

"I'm only thirteen."

"That's old enough."

She said no more. For a long time they sat in silence. Finally he said, "I made a mistake."

"That's right."

"A mistake can be undone."

"Not this one." She turned her head and looked straight at him but could not force him to meet her eye. His lip was puffy where she had struck him. "Ephraim, I can't stay here."

"So it seems." He clasped and unclasped his hands. "If you're going to be sullen and walk around with a chip on your shoulder, I'm not sure I want you around."

"You're the one who spoiled everything. We could have lived as brother and sister. You could have been like an uncle to me."

"Uncle! Will you never stop looking for somebody to take care of you?" He gave a harsh laugh. "Let's be reasonable. Suppose we have Mr. McIsaac cancel your indentures. What will you do then?"

"If I had any money, I'd go to Niagara to look for my father."

"Then that's what you ought to do. Since you haven't received an answer to your letter, it makes sense for you to go to Niagara to make your own enquiries."

"How do I get there?"

"Take the packet boat."

"That costs a lot of money."

"I intend to pay you your wages for one full year."

"I've worked here only four months."

"Mother worked you hard enough for that to count as a year. I'll take you to Kingston tomorrow. We'll visit Mr. Mc-Isaac to cancel your indentures. Then I'll book your passage on the next boat carrying passengers to Niagara. How does that sound to you?"

Everything was happening so fast that her head was in a whirl. "It sounds . . . good."

"We'll find a place for you to stay while you wait for the boat. Mr. McIsaac is certain to know some respectable woman who'd welcome a paying guest." Ephraim paused. "Is there anything I haven't thought of?"

"What about Captain?" On hearing his name, the puppy came to them, his tail wagging, and laid his head on Hope's knee. "I can take him with me, can't I?"

"Not on the packet boat. There's one big cabin for women, another for men. No place for dogs."

Hope bent her head and pressed her face against the dog's warm, coarse fur. She loved him. He was the only living creature in the whole world that loved her. She couldn't go to Niagara. She couldn't leave Captain behind.

Ephraim must have understood. "He can stay with me. I'll give him a good home."

Hope looked up. Her heart took two steps toward forgiveness. "Really?"

"Yes. Really." He stood up. "Now you go to the Andersons'

place and tell Adam he doesn't need to bring the cow today. They can keep Bossy while I take you to Kingston. Adam can return her the day after tomorrow. That way, you'll still have room to sleep in the shed one more night."

One more step toward forgiveness. Poor Ephraim. First his wife. Then his mother. He certainly had bad luck with women. His proposal had been outrageous. And yet, although she could not forgive the insult, she was beginning to sympathize with the man. Like her, he did not want to be alone. The companionship of a good dog would make up for some things lacking in his life.

CHAPTER 13

Midway through the Wood

HOPE HEARD THE COWBELL clanking before she saw Adam driving Bossy toward her along the half-made road. When he noticed her, he raised his arm in greeting. "This is a surprise. What are you doing here?" They met midway through the wood.

"I've come to save you the trouble of bringing the cow all the way to the Blocks' place and then having to take her back again. You can keep Bossy for two more days. Tomorrow Ephraim's taking me to Kingston to cancel my indentures and book my passage to Niagara."

"What!" Adam's jaw dropped. "Are you're going to Niagara

to live with your father? I didn't realize you'd found him."

"I haven't. Colonel Butler hasn't answered my letter. I'm going to Niagara to ask in person where Pa and Silas have been settled."

"Are you travelling by yourself?"

"Of course." She tried to look as if this were the most natural thing in the world.

Adam scratched his head. "Here's the girl who never left Carleton Island till she was twelve, never went to school, didn't know how to write a letter. Now she's off on her own to Niagara to speak with the commanding officer of the Nassau Militia. Four months ago I wouldn't have believed it possible."

She smiled. "With a name like Hope . . ."

He finished her sentence, ". . . anything is possible." Then his lips twisted in the half smile she knew so well. "I bet you're scared to be going all alone."

"Not a bit," she lied.

Bossy was nibbling at a clump of daisies that grew in a patch of sunshine between the trees. Adam bent over and picked a daisy. A wistful look crossed his face. "So off you go, leaving me stuck here. Ma's expecting another baby. It's going to be years before Pa can manage without me. I'll be old and grey by the time I get to go anywhere."

She picked a daisy for herself. "You never can tell what will happen. I expected to be bound for three years by my indentures. Instead, it's been four months."

"Will you ever come back?"

"No."

"So it's goodbye forever." His laugh sounded forced. "We shall never meet again."

"Well, maybe someday." She picked a petal from her daisy. "This petal says we will." She picked a second petal. "This one says we won't." Another petal. "This says we will."

"Go on. I want to know."

"This is silly. I'd never believe in anything a daisy told me." She threw the partly plucked flower onto the ground.

Adam stooped and picked it up. She looked at him holding the two daisies, the one he had picked and the one she had thrown away. He wasn't laughing now. This was how she would remember him, she thought, with his great thatch of straw-coloured hair, his big sunburned nose and his green eyes.

"So Ephraim will be left on his own," said Adam.

"Not quite. I'm leaving Captain with him." She slapped a mosquito that had landed on her wrist.

"About Ephraim," said Adam. "Ma's heard something."

"Heard something?"

"Gossip. She never goes anywhere, yet she seems to hear everything. It's as if she had antennae." He lifted his hands to his forehead and waggled his index fingers in a comic imitation of an insect testing the air.

Hope laughed, and her laughter made him smile.

"What has she heard?" Hope asked.

"It's not exactly about Ephraim. It's about his wife Philippa. Ma heard that the officer she ran away with has abandoned her."

"Really? How could your mother know that? They went to England. She couldn't hear a story like that from the far side of the Atlantic Ocean."

"Philippa never made it to England. According to Ma, the officer left her in Montreal and went home without her. It may not be true. My mother never lets the truth get in the way of a good story."

"True or not, I'm sure Ephraim hasn't heard it." Hope frowned. Or had he? And if he had, would he care?

Hope held out the switch that she used for driving the cow. "You can have this. I won't need it any longer."

He looked unimpressed with the gift; it was only a willow wand. He gave a flick aimed at the cow's backside. Bossy twitched.

"Why did you do that?" said Hope.

"I felt like it."

"It was mean."

Bossy raised her head. The large, brown eyes seemed a little less blank than usual. Hope felt a burst of affection for the cow, which, after all, had provided her with many cups of fresh milk as well as welcome opportunities to escape from Mrs. Block's bad temper. Hope rested her hand on Bossy's brow and then, on a sudden impulse, placed a kiss on her big, soft nose.

Raising her head, she saw the grin on Adam's face.

"I'd like one of those," he said.

"What?"

"A goodbye kiss."

Hope froze. "How dare you!"

Adam flinched. A deep pink flush started at his neck and rose up until his whole face was the colour of his sunburnt nose. "No offence. Just a kiss. I thought we were friends."

"We were." She turned on her heel and marched away, fuming. The whole male sex was all the same. Even Adam. She was glad she would never see him again.

Halfway back to the Blocks' place she calmed down. Maybe she had been unfair. After all, it was just a kiss. If she could kiss a cow, why not a boy? Adam had liked her, but now he would not like her any longer. She ought to go back and apologize. But what would she say? How could she explain? And so she kept on her way through the wood and back to the Blocks' cabin.

CHAPTER 14

A New Adventure

EPHRAIM'S OUTRAGEOUS PROPOSAL was not something Hope expected ever to forgive, yet her anger was beginning to cool. Without actually apologizing, he had acknowledged his fault and was making amends. Hope had noticed that some people have the ability to adapt themselves to whatever life brings their way, and he was one of those people. They go neither forward nor backwards but somehow slip sideways. Living by himself, he would make his own split-pea soup. If his soup had lumps, there would be no one to complain. She found it hard to believe that he would end up like the Squire.

When she reached the cabin, she found him standing outside the open shed door tossing dried corn to the chickens. This had been her job; now it would be his. Captain sat with his ears up and his head cocked, watching.

"I have something for you," Ephraim said as he closed the sack of corn. He led her into the cabin. From under the bunk he pulled out a small wooden trunk with brass hinges and brass corners. "This was my mother's."

Hope hesitated. The neat little trunk was a thousand times nicer than the canvas-wrapped bundle in which she had brought her possessions from the orphans' home. But should she accept it? She raised her fingers to the frill of her new mobcap. She did not trust Ephraim. Not any longer.

"No. I can't take the trunk."

"You've earned it. Consider it part of your pay. Or a bequest."

"I can manage without a trunk."

"Think what sort of impression you'll make on Colonel Butler."

That's exactly what she was thinking. Carrying her bundle, she would look like a homeless waif begging someone to take her in. It was bad enough to be wearing an orphanage gown. Maybe Ephraim was right in saying that she was at heart a practical young woman. Considering her situation, she had to be practical.

"Thank you. I'll take the trunk as part of my pay."

"Now you're showing good sense," said Ephraim.

Hope spent the rest of the day cleaning the cabin from top

to bottom. Ephraim told her not to work so hard, but she knew that she must do it in order to feel that she earned the trunk.

That night she slept in the shed for the last time. In the morning she noticed that Mrs. Block's bed had been slept in. It did not surprise her that Ephraim had taken it over, just as he had taken over the bentwood chair.

After breakfast, while he carried her trunk to the canoe, she gave Captain a hug and said goodbye. Ephraim had in-sisted that the dog stay in the cabin, not the shed, while he took her to Kingston. To leave Captain alone with the chick-ens would put too much temptation in his way.

When Hope closed the cabin door and heard him whining to go with her, her eyes filled with tears. Then Captain began to howl, and that made it even worse.

She was sniffling when she joined Ephraim at the shore. "Now what is it?" he asked her.

"Captain," she gulped. "I'll miss him so much."

"I promised you I'd take good care of him."

"I know." Her voice choked on a sob.

"Don't cry. I'll make another promise. If you ever want to take him back, he's yours."

"Thank you." Hope climbed into the canoe, and they pushed off from shore. When they were a mile beyond the Block cabin, she could still hear the dog's mournful howls. All the way to Kingston they echoed in her mind. Neither she nor Ephraim uttered a word throughout the trip.

"What's Butlersburg like?" Hope asked as they pulled up the canoe at the Kingston landing. "Is it as big as Kingston?"

"Not nearly. It's just a small village at the mouth of the Niagara River." He lifted her trunk from the bottom of the canoe and carried it by its two leather straps, one at each end. As they walked up the street, he continued his description. "Butlersburg is named for Colonel Butler. It's on the west bank, across from Fort Niagara on the east bank. Apart from Navy Hall, there are hardly any real buildings. But that may change soon. If Butlersburg becomes the centre of government for Upper Canada, it will be an interesting place to live."

"What's Upper Canada?"

He gave her a curious look. "We live in Upper Canada."

"I thought we lived in Quebec."

"Until two weeks ago, we did live in Quebec. But on August 16th a government Order-in-Council divided the Province of Quebec into Upper and Lower Canada. The western part —the part where we live—is Upper Canada."

"So one day we were in Quebec and the next day we were in Upper Canada."

"Exactly."

"Since we're still in the same place, whatever you call it, I don't see how it makes a difference."

"It makes a great deal of difference. We'll have different laws and a different government from the people who live in Lower Canada. We'll each have our own lieutenant-governor. Ours is already on his way from England. We shall have peace, order and good government. Except for the Black Loyalists in Nova Scotia, life is improving in every way."

"Black Loyalists!" Hope exclaimed. "Who are they?"

"Former slaves," said Ephraim. "England promised them freedom and land if they helped us fight the rebels. When the war ended, England kept half her promise. The Black Loyalists became free men and women. But the land they received was rocky and barren and no good for farming. Then the white population turned against them. It's a disgrace the way the Black Loyalists have been treated. Most of them want to go to Africa to live. It looks as though Britain is going to do the right thing and provide the ships so they can go there to start a new life."

"Why do they want to go to Africa?" Hope asked. "Isn't it full of elephants and tigers?"

"They think of Africa as their home, even though many of them were born in what is now the United States."

"I wish them luck," said Hope. "Everybody needs a home."

Soon they reached Mr. McIsaac's office. Since Ephraim had his hands full with the trunk, she opened the door. There sat Mr. McIsaac, with his quills and ink pot and papers arrayed in front of him. He rose from his desk. "Good morning," he said to Ephraim. "I didn't expect to see you this week."

"We've come to cancel Miss Cobman's indentures." They shook hands.

Miss Cobman! Hope liked the grown-up sound of that.

"Ah, yes," said Mr. McIsaac. "I thought you might, now that your mother has passed away." He glanced at Hope. "May I assume that you are in need of a new situation?"

"No, sir." She spoke up boldly. "I'm on my way to Niagara to look for my father. I have learned that I'll likely find him there."

"Hmm," said Mr. McIsaac. "I wish you luck. This whole country is awash with people looking for misplaced relatives." He turned again to Ephraim. "Sir, you couldn't have come at a better time. I was about to send word that I have information concerning your case. A Board of Commissioners has arrived from England to hear Loyalists' claims for compensation."

"It's about time! I was afraid I'd have to go to England to argue my case."

"That won't be necessary. The board will travel to major Loyalist centres. One is Montreal, where it will meet next week. That's why I needed to get in touch with you immediately. Unfortunately, I'm tied up with the Court of King's Bench. But I have the documents ready for you to prove your claim. I trust you will be able to go to Montreal?"

Montreal! Hope stole a sideways glance at Ephraim, but he did not look the slightest bit perturbed. There was not so much as a flicker of response when Mr. McIsaac named the city where Philippa was said to be living.

"I shall gladly make the journey," said Ephraim. "But today, let's see about those indentures. We must clear up the legalities before Miss Cobman leaves for Niagara. And if you happen to know of a suitable place where she can stay until the next packet boat sails, we would appreciate that very much."

"As it happens, I do," said Mr. McIsaac. "I have a client, Mrs. Fairley, who has a dressmaking establishment. She boards the young women apprenticed to her. One of these young women completed her apprenticeship last week. When she and Mrs. Fairley came in to sign the documents involved, Mrs. Fairley mentioned that she would have room for a paying guest until a new apprentice is bound to her next month."

Ephraim turned to Hope. "How does this sound to you?"

She nodded. "Very good." It was amazing how easily everything was falling into place.

"I'll send a message to Mrs. Fairley," said Mr. McIsaac. "Now let's see to the indentures."

After the papers cancelling the indentures were signed, Ephraim presented Hope with three pounds in Montreal money and a purse to hold her wealth. She put the purse into the pocket she wore under her gown. Next they went to a place that he called a shipping office, where he purchased a ticket for her to sail in three days on the schooner *Juliana*. The voyage to Niagara would take two days, depending on wind and weather.

Ephraim escorted her to Mrs. Fairley's establishment. It was a white frame house, two storeys high, with a sign over the door: MRS. FAIRLEY'S FINE SEWING. There was a brass knocker shaped like a lion's head on the door.

"I'll leave you here." He set down the trunk at the threshold. "I trust we part with no hard feelings."

"No hard feelings." Their eyes met, and neither looked away. "Quite otherwise, for you are helping to make my dearest dream come true." She paused. "I hope you win your case and get all that money you lost."

"Thank you." He gave a slight bow. Another first. No one had ever bowed to her before.

As he was walking away, she called to him. "Someday I may be back to claim my dog. Don't be surprised."

He stopped, turned, waved, and then continued down the street. Hope lifted the knocker and gave a sharp rap at the door.

CHAPTER 15

The Sewing Girls

THE DOOR WAS OPENED by a tall, thin woman who wore black from head to foot. Her hair was iron-grey, and she looked at Hope with steely eyes. But she was not really looking at Hope. What held her attention was the limp, shabby orphanage gown.

"Yes?" she said.

"My name is Hope Cobman. I'm the guest who's to stay with you for three days, waiting to leave on the next packet boat."

"Oh. You aren't what I expected. I'll have to speak to Mr. McIsaac about this."

So Mrs. Fairley didn't think she was good enough to occupy one of her beds. Hope straightened her shoulders. "Perhaps I should stay elsewhere if I'm not welcome here."

Mrs. Fairley's eyebrows rose. "I like a girl with spirit. Please come in." She held the door open.

Hope hoisted her trunk by its two straps and entered a hallway that had plastered walls painted green. The wide floorboards were grey. The long floor cloth was decorated with flowers and birds. A staircase to the upper storey was on the left, and a parlour on the right. The hallway ran straight through the house. Hope caught a whiff of roasting meat, at which she remembered she had not eaten since leaving the cabin that morning.

"Tabitha!" Mrs. Fairley called. A black woman wearing a blue dress with a white cap and apron appeared from the back of the house. "Take Miss Cobman's trunk to the apprentices' dormitory."

The woman obeyed. She lifted the trunk with no apparent effort and briskly trotted up the stairs.

Mrs. Fairley led Hope into the parlour and directed her to sit down. When both were seated, Mrs. Fairley said, "Upstairs there are two rooms: the sewing room and the apprentices' dormitory. I also employ two skilled seamstresses who come in by the day. All of them are now busy clearing up. So as not to disturb their work, you will wait here. Dinner will be ready in a quarter of an hour. I run a very punctual establishment. If you'll excuse me, I shall see that the cook has everything ready for Tabitha to serve." She left the parlour.

While waiting, Hope looked around. She saw a small writing desk and a side table on which stood two candlesticks, the candles unlit. There was an upholstered settee, as well as several chairs covered in needlepoint. A full-length looking glass rested in a wooden stand. The looking glass, Hope decided, was for customers to view their new finery. She stood up, crossed the floor to the looking glass and inspected her reflection. Her new white cap looked fresh and crisp, but her orphanage gown was even limper and shabbier than she had realized. No wonder Mrs. Fairley had had doubts about her suitability as a guest. Hope returned to the chair and sat down.

There was a clatter of steps on the stairs as the apprentices and the seamstresses descended. The outer door opened and closed, and then three young ladies entered the parlour. Mrs. Fairley, returning from the kitchen, introduced them.

There was Louisa, graceful and slender, wearing a dark muslin gown with a wide sash just under the gathered square neckline. She looked about seventeen years old. Agatha and Mary were younger, perhaps sixteen and fifteen respectively. Agatha, who was petite with a delicate complexion, wore a gown of yellow calico sprigged with pink flowers. Mary, the tallest although the youngest, had on a finely striped red and white gown with deep white frills on the sleeves. Each one of these garments made Hope even more painfully aware of her own dingy grey gown. Hope supposed that Louisa, Agatha and Mary had themselves sewn the charming garments that they wore.

A bell rang. It was not a gong like the bell that had assembled the orphans to dinner. This dinner bell was a tinkling cymbal. Mrs. Fairley directed the girls into the dining room in much the same way that Hope herded chickens into the shed. They said grace before sitting down.

Hope shrank in her seat and tried to make herself invisible. At the same time, she kept a careful eye on everything the others did, paying particular attention to their table manners. Hope observed how deftly they managed knife, forks and spoons and tried to do as they did, not taking a bite of anything until sure which implement it was proper to use.

"Hope is on her way to Niagara to join her father and brother," said Mrs. Fairley.

"What part of Niagara?" Louisa asked.

"Butlersburg," Hope answered.

"Butlersburg is much in the news," Mrs. Fairley said. "We thought that Kingston would be chosen as the capital of Upper Canada, but now we hear that Lieutenant-Governor Simcoe intends Butlersburg to be the centre of government. I call that a great mistake."

"Why is that?" Hope asked. Ephraim had mentioned the lieutenant-governor coming from England. Now she had an opportunity to learn what this was all about.

"Kingston has everything; Butlersburg has nothing. The capital of a province should have buildings suitable for balls

and official functions. As for providing an appropriate residence, can you imagine our lieutenant-governor being forced
to live in a tent?"

"I should think not," Hope said politely.

So far, the meal was going well. She had managed her im-
plements correctly, and she had learned that Upper Canada's
lieutenant-governor—whatever that was—bore the name
Simcoe.

Louisa spoke up. "I've heard that Mrs. Simcoe is fashion-
able and rich. I'd love to make clothes for someone like that."

"If Governor Simcoe and his lady go to Butlersburg, we'll
never have a chance," Agatha sighed.

"It's not fair," Mary murmured sadly.

Hope didn't like all this talk about gowns. She liked it even
less when Mary's attention turned to hers. "Since you are
going to Butlersburg, I wonder whether you have given any
thought to your wardrobe."

"Mary!" Mrs. Fairley's stated firmly. "That is not polite." ·

"Sorry," Mary flushed as red as the red striping of her
gown. "I just wondered because I have that gown I made last
year, and I can't wear it because I kept on growing, and it's
still as good as new. It's of no use to me. So if Hope would
like to try it on . . ."

Now all eyes turned to Hope, or at least to her gown. She
felt herself blushing too. For a moment she stared at her
plate, but then lifted her head. "What colour is it?" She forced
a smile. "I'll try it if it's anything but grey."

Everyone laughed. Even Mrs. Fairley went, "Ha! Ha! Ha!"

"It's blue," said Mary, "with white dots."

The stitching was a trifle uneven. Apologetically, Mary pointed out that this gown had been her very first creation. But a little imperfection in the stitches did not matter to Hope. The gown fit, the bodice clinging to her midriff as if it had been sewn just for her. Standing in front of the looking glass, she examined her reflection and smiled. The cornflower blue brought out the blue of her eyes. Her snub nose gave her a pert, lively look. As for her jug ears, they were not noticeable under the ruffle of her cap. Maybe she was a pretty girl, after all!

Into her trunk went the old gown, to be saved for workaday wear. She paid Mary four shillings for the gown, leaving them both well pleased with the transaction.

CHAPTER 16

Ship Ahoy!

HOPE STAYED AT MRS. FAIRLEY'S sewing establishment for three nights. On the morning of her departure, Mrs. Fairley arranged for a boy to take Hope's trunk to the harbour in a wheelbarrow. The streets were crowded. It seemed that everyone in town was heading in the same direction. There were people on foot and people on horseback and people driving wagons. The sky was blue, with a few scudding clouds. A perfect day for sailing to Niagara. Hope walked so fast that the boy with the cart had to jog to keep up.

An official wearing a green frock coat and tricorn hat appeared to be directing operations. Hope went up to him and asked where passengers were to wait.

"On the wharf." He pointed to a wooden dock where a dozen people stood amongst their boxes and trunks. The boy trundled her small trunk onto the wharf and set it down. Hope paid him one penny, which was the amount Mrs. Fairley had suggested. The boy touched the brim of his hat and then ran off, the wheel of his wheelbarrow bouncing on the rough ground.

Near Hope on the wharf stood a girl of about her age, also with a trunk at her feet. She was a plump roly-poly girl with shiny pink cheeks. Since she too was alone and obviously preparing to sail on the packet boat, Hope introduced herself and asked the girl where she was going.

"I'm Selena Morris," the girl said. "I'm going to Niagara to join my family. I haven't seen them for seven years, and I'm *so* excited!"

"What happened to keep you apart for so long?"

"It's because of the war. We were Georgia Loyalists. When the rebels took over Savannah, I became separated from my family during the evacuation. It was chaos. People were so desperate to escape that they were pushing each other out of the harbour boats that were carrying Loyalists to the British ships. There were dozens of ships and dozens of boats. The boat my family was in was overcrowded, so another came to take some people off. I was huddled on the floor of the first boat, on my hands and knees in water, and so terrified I couldn't move. My mother thought my father had me. My father thought my mother did. They got into the second boat, but I didn't."

"How could they fail to notice you weren't with them?"

"They had their hands full," said Selena. "Mama had my baby sister in her arms. Papa had my two little brothers to look after, as well as our boxes. I was seven years old. If I hadn't been terrified, I would have had the sense to stick close to them." She shrugged. "But I didn't. So that's how it happened. The boat I was in went to one ship, and the boat with the rest of my family went to another."

"And then?" Hope asked.

"When the boat I was in reached the ship, I looked around for my parents to help me up the ladder. When I didn't see them, I was more scared than ever. I remember a man shouting, 'Hurry up!' Somebody gave me a hand climbing the ladder. The deck was swarming with people. I was running around bawling and asking if anyone had seen my mama and papa. Nobody had. A family named Doyle took me under their wing and comforted me. They looked after me all through the voyage. They had a boy and a girl close to my age. They told me that most of the evacuation ships were going to East Florida. Uncle Ned—Mr. and Mrs. Doyle asked me to call them Uncle Ned and Aunt Sally—said that when we reached East Florida, we'd be sure to find my parents. But we didn't."

"Where had their ship gone?"

"To Jamaica. But we didn't know that. Most of the ships had gone to East Florida, but a few had gone to the West Indies."

"So you were in East Florida and your family was in Jamaica."

"That's right. Neither knew where the other was. Uncle Ned and Aunt Sally didn't like the climate in East Florida. After a couple of years, we left. We went first to Nova Scotia, and then moved west to Kingston. The Doyles treated me like one of their own children, but I kept the name Morris. We all hoped that someday I'd be reunited with my real family.

"If my real family had stayed in Jamaica, I likely never would see them again. But my father is a merchant. He saw an opportunity to do business provisioning British forts. That's what took him to Niagara. People go back and forth all the time between Niagara and Kingston. After a while, somebody put the two stories together: little girl lost her parents; parents lost their little girl. So here I am."

By the time Selena had finished her story, the harbour boat had left shore to fetch the passengers disembarking at Kingston. They were assembled on the deck of the *Juliana* with their boxes and trunks. The first person to leave the ship was an official carrying a black box with the words Royal Mail in shiny brass letters. The passengers then descended the ladder and seated themselves on the benches in the harbour boat. The sailors followed with the luggage.

When the boat reached the wharf, it was again the official with the box of mail who was helped out first. He did not release his hold on the box at any time. Hope was glad to see him take such good care of the Royal Mail. It made her feel more confident that her letter had indeed reached Colonel Butler.

Now it was time to embark. But before anyone else got into the harbour boat, the official returned carrying a box that looked the same as the one he had taken from the ship. The passengers did not climb into the harbour boat until he was seated. A cheerful young sailor helped Hope and Selena step from the wharf into the boat.

"At last I'm on my way!" Hope said to herself as the boat pulled away from the wharf. Selena sat beside her, her dimpled hands clasped tightly on her lap. She glanced back over her shoulder several times in the direction of the throng of people standing on the shore.

It took only a few minutes for the boat to reach the *Juliana*. As Hope climbed up the ship's ladder, she was careful to keep any speck of dust or tar from touching her new gown. When all were aboard and the *Juliana* was ready to leave the harbour, Selena asked, "Will you watch my box while I wave goodbye to the Doyles?"

"Gladly."

Selena rushed to the railing and began waving to the crowd on the waterfront. She did not stop waving until the schooner had left Kingston Harbour. When she rejoined Hope, she had tears in her eyes. "I'm going to miss them," she sniffed. "For half my life they've been my family." Hope sympathized, but only up to a point. It was hard to feel sorry for a girl who had not just one but *two* loving families.

CHAPTER 17

Swinging a Cot

SELENA WIPED HER EYES and gave one more sniff. "Let's go below," she said, quickly recovering her spirits. "We must claim our cots. I don't want the spot next to the wall."

Hope didn't know what Selena was talking about, but she followed her to the hatch and down a set of steep stairs that was little more than a ladder. A sailor helped them with their trunks, bumping them down from step to step.

At the bottom of the stairs there were two doors facing each other across a corridor. A sign on one door stated, "Female Passengers." The sign on the other door read, "Male Passengers." When Selena opened the door of the cabin reserved for females, Hope saw a roomful of hammocks hung side by side from hooks screwed into the timbers on opposite walls. The hammocks were so close together that they almost touched.

"See what I mean?" said Selena. "The last ship I was on, there was scarcely room to swing a cot. I had the spot next to the wall, so every time the ship gave a toss, I was flung against the wall. By the time we had sailed from St. Augustine to Saint John, I was black and blue."

"So that's what you call a cot," said Hope. "I thought a cot was a bed with foldable legs."

"On a ship, a cot is a long skinny net you sleep in. When nobody else is around, it's fun to swing a cot." Selena grabbed the side of a hammock, and sprang up like a bouncing ball. "Want to try it? Climb into the cot next to mine."

Hope followed her example, though her less practised leap almost sent her catapulting over the hammock to the other side.

As soon as they were ensconced, Selena gave Hope's cot a shove. "If we push and pull, we can get them swinging so fast you think we'll turn upside down." Hope wasn't sure this was a good idea, but she was willing to try it.

Soon they had the two cots swinging in unison, faster and faster, higher and higher. Selena shrieked with laughter. Hope, clutching both sides, felt her stomach lurch.

Then the door opened. The woman who entered the cabin gave a gasp. "Good heavens! Are you trying to break your necks? This is no way for young girls to behave."

The man who followed her remained only long enough to set down a trunk before retreating.

Hope gladly let her cot come to rest. She peeped over the edge. The woman had beady eyes, a tiny mouth and a double chin that quivered with indignation. "You are behaving like a pair of monkeys swinging in the trees," she said and, without waiting for a response, left the cabin.

"I'd like to be a monkey swinging in a tree," said Selena. "There's not much to do on a voyage. I'd rather swing than play whist." She sat up and looked at Hope. "You're white as a ghost. Didn't you like swinging your cot?"

"Not very much. At the top of the swing, I was afraid I'd fall out."

"You wouldn't. But that doesn't matter. If you don't wish to swing, you don't have to. I want to hear your story. So far, I've done all the talking."

Hope lay still for a minute, arranging her thoughts and letting her stomach settle. "It's like this." She began at the beginning with her father's going off to war before her mother knew that another child was on the way. She told Selena about her birth in the forest, her childhood in the barracks, her year at the orphanage and the four months she spent looking after Mrs. Block. She ended with her plan to search for her father and her brother Silas at Niagara.

Selena listened attentively, with only the occasional gasp of sympathy to interrupt the story. When Hope had finished, she said, "You're brave to set out on your own, especially since you aren't even sure you're going to find them. And if you do find them, what if you don't like them? I mean, they'll be total strangers."

"Selena, I'm going to find them, and I'm going to love them, just as they're going to love me. I know this the same way that I know the sun will rise tomorrow."

"I still think you're brave," said Selena.

After a few minutes they went on deck. For the rest of the day, they watched the forest go by, mile after mile of green trees broken up by small farms and the occasional settlement. An awning had been rigged up on the deck for passengers who wanted to keep out of the sun. Sailors carried up from the galley steaming kettles of beans simmered in molasses, a stack of hardtack biscuits and a cauldron of tea. Some passengers had come aboard with their own food in wicker hampers. People sat under the awning to eat, as if it were a picnic.

Hope and Selena remained on deck until the stars came out, and then they went below. They were the youngest of the six female passengers. Only a few years their elder was a bride on her way to join her husband. He was, she said, a corporal in the 24th Regiment of Foot stationed at Fort Niagara. She told them that only a few men were allowed to have their wives with them. She was happy to be one of the lucky few, although she did not look forward to her work as a laundress for the soldiers.

There was also a quiet woman of middle years who impressed Hope with the elaborateness of her blue bonnet, which had a tall crown bound about with a wide silk ribbon and surmounted by an indigo plume that was two feet long.

The oldest was a white-haired woman, who let the others know that she was on her way to visit her daughter in Queenston.

The sixth female passenger was the stern woman who disapproved of girls swinging cots.

Selena was eager to share her story with the others, but Hope remained silent, for she did not feel like speaking of her quest again.

Before long, all talking ceased. The cots swayed gently in unison as the *Juliana* held its steady course.

Hope lay awake, thinking about her father and Silas, but mainly about her father. Shutting out everything except the motion of the cot, she summoned from the depths of her mind the man whom she had spent her whole life imagining. Tall and thin. Brown eyes, black hair and bushy eyebrows. The smell of pipe tobacco. He regarded her tenderly, his arms ready to hug her. She went to sleep waiting for him to speak her name.

During the night the wind dropped. When Hope went up on deck in the morning, she saw that the *Juliana* was not going anywhere. She rested at anchor near the mouth of a creek where a band of Indians was camped. Their bark-covered lodges looked like overturned mixing bowls with a hole on top.

To pass the time, one of the male passengers brought his fiddle up on deck. He played "Devil's Dream," "The Girl I Left behind Me" and "The World Turned Upside Down."

The ship was close enough to shore for the Indians to hear the music. They must have liked it, for two of them came out in a canoe with a big basket of fresh fish, which they offered as a gift. The ship's cook said he would fry it up for the passengers. Though a few passengers complained of the delay that resulted from being becalmed, most saw it as part of a traveller's lot and treated it as a holiday. Hope had not had such a pleasant time for as long as she could remember.

That night a fresh wind filled the sails again. In the morning, when Hope and Selena went on deck, the ship had reached the mouth of a steep-banked river. On the east bank stood a huge fortress. On the west side of the river there was a village. A man standing near Hope exclaimed to his companion, "See that cloud of mist rising in the distance? That's the spray of the Falls." So this was Niagara. They had arrived.

Clinging to the railing, Selena hopped up and down with excitement, her round cheeks deep pink as she waved to the throng gathered on the wharf.

Hope joined her at the railing. "Do you see your family?"

The question was unnecessary. There could be no doubt about whom Selena was waving to. Two stocky little boys were holding between them a white banner on which was written "Welcome Home Selena." A chubby little girl was dancing about. A man and a woman, the latter short and plump, waved energetically.

The ship moored at the wharf. The gangplank was lowered. After giving Hope a hug, Selena rushed ashore. Hope hung back as a surge of loneliness swept over her. People of all ages were smiling and embracing. If only someone were there to welcome her!

Then suddenly she saw a tall man with bushy eyebrows smiling in her direction. There he stood, one hand waving and the other holding a bunch of flowers. Had her wish been granted? For one delirious moment, it seemed that by some miracle her father had come to meet her.

Yet all she had to do was turn her head to see that the object of the man's attention was the person right behind her on the gangway. It was the quiet woman with the elaborate blue bonnet. She was waving to the man, the plume on her bonnet ducking and rising. Her eyes shone with happiness, and on the man's face was an expression of equal joy. They rushed toward one another. At the bottom of the gangway, Hope had to dodge to avoid their embrace.

After that, she did not feel so much disappointed as foolish while she waited for the sailors to bring her trunk off the ship. Even after it had been brought to her, she lingered on the wharf looking about. Before anything else, she had to find someone who could take her to Colonel Butler. It sounded simple enough, but she didn't know where to start.

CHAPTER 18

Navy Hall

AFTER THE OTHER PASSENGERS had been taken away by families and friends and the sailors had returned to the ship, Hope remained on the wharf. She sat down on her trunk, wondering what to do next, when a freckle-faced boy with a wheelbarrow came her way. He said, "Do you need someone to carry your box?"

She hesitated. Her trunk was small enough for her to carry for a short distance, but she did not know how far she had to go. "I might if I knew where I was going."

The boy lifted one eyebrow. "You must have some idea."

"I have to see Colonel Butler of the Nassau Militia."

"He's likely at Navy Hall. For a penny, I'll take you there."

She had money in her purse, the coins safe in the pocket that she wore under her gown, fastened by straps to a belt around her waist. When she put her hand on her side, it was reassuring to feel its shape.

"Is it far?"

He pointed to a cluster of wooden buildings. "That's Navy Hall."

It was too far to walk while carrying her trunk. "Yes," she told the boy, "I will hire you."

After the boy had loaded her trunk into his wheelbarrow, they started off. It took only a short time to reach Navy Hall. The boy stopped the first redcoat they met.

"Can you tell me where we'll find Colonel Butler?"

The soldier motioned toward a two-storey, gambrel-roof structure that looked like a barracks. "Over there."

Hope followed the boy to the building. He picked up her trunk, carried it inside and set it on a bench outside a closed door. The penny paid and the boy gone, she sat down on the bench. From inside the door came two male voices in earnest conversation. She had no choice but to hear them.

"I don't mind if he changes the name," came the deeper voice. "I'm proud of it, but whoever heard of a capital called Butlersburg? It lacks dignity. If Simcoe wants to call the town Newark, that's all right with me." He paused. "Mr. Hamilton, you and I have more important matters to worry about."

"Such as where he's going to live." Mr. Hamilton had a Scottish accent.

"Precisely," said the deeper voice. "We have no residence

suitable for a lieutenant-governor, and no hope of having one built before next summer."

"Well, Colonel, maybe we can modify part of Navy Hall." This was the man called Mr. Hamilton. "If we can't make it vice regal, at least we can make it comfortable."

"That's likely the best solution."

Chair legs scraped on the floor, footsteps approached and the voices came nearer. The door opened, and a middle-aged gentleman wearing a ruffled shirt and blue velvet frock coat came out. Without glancing in Hope's direction, he left the building.

Hope jumped to her feet and turned to face the man who stood at the open door. He had piercing eyes and white hair—not powdered, but actually white. He was old, yet not stooped. His shoulders were squared and his posture erect. In his red coat with its gold epaulets and yards of gold braid, he looked the way a colonel ought to look.

"Excuse me," said Hope. "Are you Colonel Butler?"

"I am."

"May I please speak with you?"

He was already closing the door, but he stopped and looked at her. "May I ask the reason?"

"My name is Hope Cobman. I wrote you a letter."

"Many people write me letters."

"It was about my father Sergeant John Cobman and my brother Private Silas Cobman. I've come to Niagara to find them."

"Oh," said Colonel Butler. "I remember the letter." He motioned her to enter and closed the door. "Please take a seat."

There was a big mahogany desk in the room, but he did not sit down at it. Instead, he pulled up a chair and sat facing her. "Yes, I recall the letter." He spoke slowly, his tone courteous. Hope realized that he was trying to make her feel comfortable, and his thoughtfulness put her at ease. "I gave it to Sergeant Cobman himself," said the colonel, "assuming he would contact you."

"He never did."

"I'm sorry." Colonel Butler put his hand on his brow, then pulled his fingers through his hair. "I should have answered your message, if only to tell you that I gave the letter to your father. But I have been extremely busy. As you may know, Newark is to be the seat of government for Upper Canada. We have no suitable buildings to house the Legislature and the Law Courts. We have no fit residence for the lieutenant-governor. We have no church for the clergyman who is already on his way from England to minister to us. To add to the pressure, today's packet boat brought word that there will be a royal visit next summer by Prince Edward, Duke of Kent."

Hope stirred uneasily in her chair. "With all those important things to look after, it's no wonder you don't have time to spend on such a small matter as this."

"No small matter!" His tone deepened. "Nothing is more important to me than the welfare of the men I led in battle.

They lost everything by joining my Rangers. Their property was seized, and they'll be hanged as traitors if they're ever caught in the United States. That's why I spare no effort in helping them settle in Niagara so they can begin a new life for themselves, as your father is doing."

"And my brother Silas?"

"I'm sorry to give you sad news." Colonel Butler bowed his head. "By the time we fought our last battle, nine hundred men had served in my regiment. Some Rangers I do not clearly remember. But I remember Silas." The pitch of Colonel Butler's voice was low and measured, yet gave a suggestion that he was familiar with grief. "My son Walter was his commanding officer. They died the same day. October 30, 1781, during a clash with rebel troops, crossing a ford at West Canada Creek."

Hope clasped her hands together. "So I have lost a brother whom I never met. Silas went off to war before I was born."

Colonel Butler leaned slightly toward her, and she saw the sympathy in his eyes. "Bad things happen in war. Soldiers die. Even those who live can be badly damaged."

Hope started. Did the colonel know about Elijah?

"What do you mean?" she asked.

"Your father. You have to understand."

"Was my father . . . damaged?"

"He did not escape unscathed, although others were worse afflicted." Colonel Butler rose to his feet. "Come. You want to find him. I'll have one of my young officers escort you. Ensign Dunn will enjoy the assignment." He crossed the room to pull the bell cord.

"I have a small trunk," said Hope.

"Leave it here for the time being. When you know where you'll be staying, it can be sent on. Truth to tell, it's hard to guess how your father will receive you."

"Please tell me how he received the letter."

"He was surprised. I remember how he unfolded the paper and ran his eyes over it. Then he looked up and said, 'I have no daughter.' My answer was, 'The lady seems to think you do.' He replied that he would take care of the matter. But it seems he never did."

"I see." Hope stood up. Before she could think what to say next, a young officer entered the room, making a fine appearance in his scarlet coat with its shiny silver buttons. His was a very young face, with smooth skin and pink cheeks. He would be, Hope thought, an agreeable companion.

"Miss Cobman," the colonel said, "may I present Ensign Godfrey Dunn." His formality made her feel very grown up, especially when Ensign Dunn responded with a bow before standing stiffly at attention to receive his orders. He was to escort Hope to a particular location three miles away, up the Niagara River, overlooking the gorge, and he was to attend her until she had no further need for his services.

"Very good, sir," said Ensign Dunn.

She shared this opinion. Hope did not know what lay ahead, but she felt stronger not to be facing it alone.

CHAPTER 19

Too Close to the Brink

ENSIGN GODFREY DUNN CLEARLY enjoyed his assignment. He kept pointing out things for Hope to admire. A bald eagle soaring over the canyon. A swallowtail butterfly on a twig. The wild grapevines trailing their bunches of dusty, blue fruit. He named the trees they were passing: oak, ash, maple, chestnut, hickory and black walnut. Hope tried to show a proper degree of interest, but her mind was too much on the coming meeting with her father.

The road followed the course of the river, edging at times uncomfortably close to the very brink of the Niagara Gorge.

"I'd hate to have to walk along this road in the dark," said Hope.

"There have been a few accidents," her escort said, "usually after too many drinks at the Butlersburg tavern. I see how careful you are not to venture close to the edge. Are you afraid of heights?"

"I suppose I must be, but I didn't know it until now. I've never before seen a cliff as steep as this."

"There's nothing to fear. The rock is solid limestone. We can walk right to the edge to give you a good look."

"I . . . I . . . I'm in a hurry to get to my father's home."

"This won't take a minute." He offered the crook of his elbow. "You can take my arm if you're nervous."

"I'm not nervous." She rejected his elbow, followed him to the brink and peered over.

At the bottom of the cliff, the dark river ran far below. Massive slabs of fallen rock lay along its banks. As Hope looked down, a wave of fear washed over her and she felt the bottom of the gorge lifting toward her. There was a roaring in her ears. She took a step forward.

A firm hand grabbed her arm. "Whoa! Steady there!"

"What?" She lifted her eyes from the abyss.

"I thought you were going to faint."

She shook her head to clear away the dizziness. "I don't know what came over me."

He led her back to the roadside. "I do apologize," he said. "I didn't intend to frighten you like that."

"It was such a queer feeling. I wanted to jump. I couldn't help myself."

"There's a word for how you felt: vertigo. I advise you to stay away from heights."

He released her arm, and they walked on. Hope's experience at the edge of the gorge seemed to have affected him, for he stopped pointing out interesting things to look for in that direction.

As soon as her panic subsided, she turned her thoughts again to the coming meeting with her father. What Colonel Butler had said alarmed her, especially his description of her father's reaction to the letter. He had said to Colonel Butler, "I have no daughter." Maybe she was making a mistake. What if she was following a will-o'-the-wisp leading her to some place where she did not want to go? But it was too late to turn back, even if she wanted to. And she did not want to turn back. *If Pa thinks he has no daughter*, she resolved, *I'll just have to change his mind.*

"There it is!" Ensign Dunn's voice broke in upon her thoughts. He pointed to a log cabin at the end of an overgrown path. Its appearance was not reassuring. It looked in bad shape. The mud and moss used to plug the gaps between the logs seemed to be washing out. Two small windows flanked the plank door. One window was boarded over.

"Is this it?" she asked. "Does Sergeant Cobman really live there?"

The young ensign flushed, as if embarrassed not to have

something better to show her. "I don't want to be in your way," he said. "I'll just walk around and look for butterflies until you're finished." He added by way of explanation, "I'm making a catalogue of the different kinds."

As Hope stepped onto the rickety step in front of the door, a rattlesnake slithered underneath. She raised her fist to knock, hoping that she looked less nervous than she felt. She drew two deep breaths to quiet her thumping heart. Then she knocked.

She heard footsteps, followed by a bump, as if someone had stumbled.

The man who opened the door was not what she had expected. His hair and his eyebrows were grey, not black. She knew he would be thin, but not this thin. His cheeks were sunken. His brown eyes gleamed with the same feverish brightness she had seen in her mother's eyes. He had the same pallor. For one shocked moment Hope froze where she stood.

"Yes?" he said gruffly.

She opened her mouth, but her words stuck in her throat.

"What is it you want?" he asked.

She forced out the words. "I'm your daughter."

He shook his head from side to side. "I have no daughter."

"Colonel Butler says you read my letter."

"Yes, I read it. I'm John Cobman and Silas was my son. But I'm not your father."

He stood in the open doorway, one hand on the door,

ready to close it. She took a step toward him. With her face raised, tilted to meet his gaze, he could not fail to see her snub nose and blue eyes.

His eyes widened. He stared at her. A long time seemed to pass before he said another word. His voice shook. "For sure, you're Sadie Cobman's daughter. You'd be a twin to her at that age." He gave a deep, rattling cough. "But that doesn't mean you're a child of mine. I don't know why she sent you here, but—"

"Nobody sent me. Ma died more than a year ago."

He dropped his hand from the door. "Sadie dead! May God have mercy on her soul." He bowed his head for only a moment and then raised it. "So it's all your own idea. The letter. This visit." He looked at Hope pityingly. "I'm beginning to understand the reason for your search. It's because you have no one. You're alone in the world. Like me." He opened the door wider. "Will you come in?"

CHAPTER 20

Twists and Turns

HE OPENED THE DOOR WIDER, and she entered. The cabin was small, approximately ten feet by ten. By the light that came through the unbroken window she saw an unmade bed with a filthy blanket on top, two wooden chairs and a table. There was a plank floor that looked as if it had not been swept for months. Two shelves were built into the cabin wall. On the upper shelf, which was on a level with Hope's head, she saw a Bible and writing materials. On the lower shelf were tin plates, bowls and cups, none of which looked clean. The air was foul with the stench of stale sweat, dirty clothes and sickness.

He held out a chair at the table for her. When she was seated, he walked unsteadily to the opposite side of the table and lowered himself into the chair facing hers. "Look," he said. A spasm of coughing seized him. He hacked noisily and then spat into a bloody cloth he held to his mouth. The blood, the coughing, the dirt and the smell all combined to make Hope feel queasy. "Look," he repeated, "I don't want to be too hard on your mother. I haven't been a saint all my life. No reason to think Sadie would be any different." He wiped a dribble of blood from the corner of his mouth. "I can understand how she got friendly with somebody else while I was away fighting for King George. These things happen."

Hope's brain reeled. She could not believe that her father would say such a thing about her mother. Pressure mounted in her head, a throbbing at her temples. Then disbelief turned to rage. She stood up and leaned forward, glaring at him.

"No! Ma wasn't like that. She never loved any man but you. She talked about you all the time." Hope stepped back from the table, knocking over her chair. "I won't listen to you speak about Ma that way. I'm leaving right now."

He started to rise, bracing himself with both hands planted on the table top, then sank back into his seat. He sat with his eyes closed. His skin looked greasy with sweat.

Hope stared. "Are you all right?" A foolish question. Of course he wasn't.

He gasped. "Wooden bucket under the shelf. Bring me water."

She found the bucket and looked inside. It was empty. "You're out of water. Where's your well? I'll fetch some."

"My well's gone bad. I've been using my neighbour's. Shaw's place. Lot next to mine . . . up the river." He tried again to stand but again crumpled into his chair.

In an instant she was out the door.

Ensign Dunn, his head bent over, was staring raptly at a bush or at something in the bush. Right now she did not want to talk to anybody. The bucket bumping against her leg, she raced down the path to the road and then turned right, heading upriver.

The road was narrow and the cliff was steep. Hope stayed as far from the edge as she could. She did not have far to go. The neighbour's cabin stood at the end of a path that ran north from the road. Halfway up the path was the well. There was a dry stone wall two courses high around the dug hole. Beside it lay a coiled rope and a smooth rock the size of a baby's head. Hope tied the rope to the handle of the bucket and placed the rock inside. The water was about six feet down. It looked clear. She lowered the bucket. With the rock to make it sink, the bucket quickly filled.

Bringing it up was the hard part. Maybe she should have taken Ensign Dunn away from his butterflies. But she managed to haul up the bucket, hand over hand. With a feeling of satisfaction she untied the rope and plunged her hands into the cool water to remove the rock. The bucket was two-thirds full. Enough water to last her father for a few days.

She was coming up the path to the cabin when Ensign Dunn saw her, tilted to one side by the weight of the bucket. He ran to her and took the bucket from her hand. "Why didn't you ask me to go with you? My assignment was to help you, not chase butterflies."

She had no suitable answer. "I wish I had," she said meekly. "He asked for water, and from the way he looked, I knew his need was great. He told me his well was bad."

"Very bad. I saw it," said Ensign Dunn, "and I smelled it. It stinks like rotten eggs and there's a dead raccoon half sunk. It's been dead a long time."

At the door she stopped and took the bucket from him. "I won't be long."

Her father had somehow got himself onto the bed. He was lying on his side, shaking with fever.

"I'm back," she said. She found the dipper, filled it with water and brought it to the bedside. Hope knew how to manage this part. She had done it for her mother so many times, raising her with one arm around her shoulders while holding the dipper to her mouth. It felt right to be doing the same for her father. He needed her. She could take care of him. But he did not want her, and there was nothing she could do about that.

When he had finished drinking, he lay back resting, his eyes fixed on her. She sat beside him, hands clasped in her lap. After a time, she saw the flicker of a smile, and then the look on his face that she had dreamed of. Tender. Full of Concern. Fatherly.

"You'd best go back where you came from," he said. "There's nothing I can do for you. I hope you'll find your father. If I had any advice on where to look, I'd tell you. But I haven't. And so I wish you well."

She squeezed his hand and then stood up. "Goodbye."

Ensign Dunn was sitting on the step when she left the cabin. He stood and held out his hand. She took it. Because her knees were shaking, she did not let go of his hand.

"He doesn't believe that I'm his daughter. I can't stay here."

"Shall I take you back to Butlersburg?"

"Yes, please."

Neither Hope nor Ensign Dunn spoke for a long time. They were nearing Navy Hall before she let go of his hand. Hope asked, "How long will I have to wait for the next packet boat?"

"Only until tomorrow. It will be the same ship that brought you here. The Niagara River is navigable only as far as Queenston. That's where cargo is unloaded for the portage around Niagara Falls. Everything going to Detroit or to the settlements on Lake Erie has to be taken off the ship at Queenston, transported overland and then loaded onto a different ship at Fort Erie. When the *Juliana*'s been unloaded, she'll sail back to Butlersburg to pick up mail and passengers for her return voyage to the eastern end of Lake Ontario."

"I'll be on that boat," said Hope. "I'll book my passage this afternoon and then find somewhere to stay for one night. There's an inn, I suppose?"

"It's rough and dirty. You wouldn't want to stay there. I

know a better place. It's the home of a widow, Mrs. Hill, who belongs to our church. I mean, we don't actually have a church, but we meet for worship. I'm sure Mrs. Hill will take you in." He hesitated. "I don't intend to be impertinent . . . I mean, it's not any of my business—"

"Thank you, Mr. Dunn. I appreciate your help."

Hope did not care where she slept that night, so long as there was a roof over her head.

CHAPTER 21

The Kindness of Strangers

AT NAVY HALL, Hope booked her passage to Milltown. She had no clear plan for her future, beyond showing up at Charlotte's door. After that, she would work it out step by step.

The ticket purchased, she and Ensign Dunn walked to the home of Mrs. Hill. It was a short distance outside Butlersburg, a two-storey white frame house with black shutters. A pair of lilac bushes flanked the front door. Ensign Dunn knocked at the door.

Hope felt jittery waiting for his knock to be answered. As she listened to footsteps approaching, she half expected a raging demon of a woman—somebody worse than Mrs. Block—to scream at her to go away.

But the woman who answered the door had a smiling face. Her voice was soft, with a friendly tone as she greeted Ensign Dunn and was introduced to Hope. She was, she said, delighted to meet Miss Cobman. Her smile faded as Ensign Dunn explained the reason Hope needed a place to stay.

"Ah, you poor girl," she said, laying a hand on her arm. "You have been through a very difficult time. Come in and have a cup of tea. You too, Godfrey. You must both be thirsty from all that walking."

She led the way to her kitchen, where a kettle steamed on the fireplace hob. They sat down at the plain, board table. When the tea was ready, Mrs. Hill poured for them. Then she produced shortbread from a tin. Hope was grateful that Mrs. Hill made no further mention of her plight. They discussed Hope's voyage on the packet boat, a journey that Mrs. Hill had made several times in order to visit a sister who lived in Kingston.

By the time two cups of tea and a plateful of shortbread had been consumed, Hope and Godfrey had abandoned formal titles. She was no longer Miss Cobman to him, nor was he Ensign Dunn to her. The world began to seem a better place. As long as they kept on talking and eating in Mrs. Hill's cozy kitchen, Hope could keep thoughts of her father at bay.

While Godfrey was gone to fetch Hope's trunk from Navy Hall, Mrs. Hill took her upstairs to the room that would be hers for the night. It was simply furnished: a bed, a bedside table, a wardrobe, a washstand with a china pitcher and bowl.

"I hope you'll be comfortable here," said Mrs. Hill.

"I certainly shall," said Hope, warmed by the woman's kindness. She did not mention that this was the first time in her life that she would have a bedroom to herself for even one night.

"Until supper is ready," said Mrs. Hill, "you might like to rest."

"Can't I help you?"

"Of course, if you aren't too tired."

Hope was tired, but she did not want to be alone with her thoughts. "I'd rather keep busy," she said.

Mrs. Hill sent Hope to her back garden to pull a few carrots. It was a neat little garden, with carrots and potatoes growing in straight rows, and sprawling vines of squash and melons, some nearly ready to be picked. There were two peach trees, the pink and yellow fruit bowing their slender branches.

Dusk was gathering when Godfrey returned with Hope's trunk. He could not stay, but left promptly to report to Colonel Butler that his mission was complete. "I look forward to meeting you again," he told Hope, "under happier circumstances."

"I do too. But even if we never meet again, I'll not forget your kindness."

"I am happy to have been of service." He bowed.

Supper was simple: ham, potatoes and carrots, followed by sliced peaches and tea. Hope filled her bedroom pitcher with water from the well to carry up to her room. After she had undressed and washed, she climbed into bed and blew out her candle.

Suddenly, in the darkness her father's face was before her, and she heard again his words, "I have no daughter."

It was as simple as that. She had his sympathy. He wished her well. But sympathy and good wishes did not fill the terrible emptiness she felt within. She rolled over and sobbed into her pillow.

Then she felt anger rising through her grief. *It's finished,* she told herself. *If he doesn't have a daughter, then I don't have a father. I'm not going to cry for him again.*

Hope closed her eyes, determined not to shed another tear. She willed herself to sleep, but her thoughts and feelings were in such a jumble, such a mingling of heartbreak and anger, that she knew she would be awake all night.

All of a sudden it was morning. Hope blinked at the light that came through the crack in the shutters and raised herself on one elbow. She had been so sure that she would be unable to sleep! It seemed that she had been more tired than she had realized.

Downstairs, Mrs. Hill was clattering about preparing breakfast. Hope sprang out of bed, washed and hurried to get dressed. When she came downstairs, Mrs. Hill had the table set. "It's just toast and tea," she apologized. "I can't get eggs. The garrison buys up all that the local farmers can produce."

Mrs. Hill was kind and calm. She talked about the weather and about the preparations for Lieutenant-Governor Simcoe's arrival the following summer. It was only after they had finished breakfast and Hope was about to leave that she said, "I am truly sorry that you find yourself in this plight."

"Thank you," said Hope. She appreciated Mrs. Hill's sympathy and was deeply grateful for her hospitality, yet she did not want to talk about her father.

Mrs. Hill spoke again, "It is hard to be alone in the world. I remember well. My mother and father died in the same week during a cholera epidemic when I was fifteen. I almost wished that I could die, too. I was terrified that I'd be begging my bread from door to door and sleeping in the streets. But I survived, and so will you."

As Mrs. Hill turned her face away, it struck Hope that she found it hard to talk about this. Again she thanked her. When she asked what she should pay for the night's lodging, Mrs. Hill said firmly that there would be no charge.

She gave Hope a piece of rope to tie around the leather handles of her trunk, one at each end. This made it possible for her to carry her trunk on her back. Hope was glad to do this. Despite the discomfort, she liked the idea that she could carry her burden herself.

At Navy Hall she learned that the *Juliana* was expected back from Queenston at noon and would sail from Butlersburg before sunset if the wind was right.

There was one last thing she wanted to do before leaving,

and that was to thank Colonel Butler for his help and to tell him about her meeting with her father. When she knocked at his door at Navy Hall, he opened it promptly and invited her to enter.

He gestured that she should take a seat, and when she was settled in a chair, he sat facing her. "Ensign Dunn told me what happened. I was sorry, but not surprised."

"You prepared me for disappointment," she said. "It could have been worse. He was kind to me, although I could not make him change his mind."

"Didn't you ever wonder," the colonel asked, "why your father didn't look for your mother after the war ended? It was seven years ago."

"I always supposed he didn't know where to look. He couldn't return to Canajoharie, where my family used to live. As a Loyalist who had fought for King George, he'd be killed if he went there. Even if he did risk it, nobody in Canajoharie would know where my mother had gone."

"True," said Colonel Butler, "but he must have been aware of an easier way to find her. If she was registered as a Loyalist refugee living at one of the border forts, it would not have been difficult."

"You mean, he didn't try."

"When a war ends, most soldiers want to return to their families and pick up their lives where they left off. But sometimes a man has been changed into a different person, and he can't face pretending to be the person he used to be. Some men in this situation take off for Indian territory. In your father's case, his way of escape was simply to stay right here."

Colonel Butler stood up. "Now you must excuse me. I have a meeting to attend."

She rose, and as he opened the door for her, he said, "At least you've seen him. I hope that's some consolation. You are young. It's time to get on with the rest of your life."

CHAPTER 22

Trouble Underfoot

HOPE WAS RAISING her fist to knock on the Schylers' door when a clear treble voice rang out from somewhere above.

"Did you come to see Mama again?"

She looked up. There was young Isaac in the apple tree in the front yard, straddling a branch six feet over her head. Amidst the green leaves and red apples she saw a pair of bright blue eyes and a thatch of blond hair.

"I'm a monkey," he said.

"Yes. I see that you're a monkey." She resisted the temptation to tell him to be careful climbing trees.

At Hope's knock, Charlotte opened the door.

"Hope! Come in! You've no idea how glad I am to see you."

This was good news to Hope, who had been feeling lonely and unwanted ever since leaving Niagara. As soon as Hope had stepped inside and set down her trunk, Charlotte gave her a hug. With her mouth close to Hope's ear, she whispered, "Elijah's here."

"What!" Hope's hand flew up to cover her mouth.

"He showed up three days ago. Sit down. I'll make tea. Then I'll tell you about it."

Hope pulled up a chair at the long wooden table while Charlotte made tea. Baby Joan was asleep in her cradle. Martha and Jack were playing with wooden animals on the braided rug that covered half the floor. They greeted their mother's visitor politely and then returned to what interested them more.

When the tea was ready, Charlotte sat down across the table from Hope. She leaned forward. "He's under the floor." She spoke so quietly that Hope could barely hear her words.

Hope whispered, "In your root cellar?"

"We don't have a root cellar. He's right under us. Nick sawed a floor plank in two places so a length can be lifted out. He made the cuts under the table, where they wouldn't be noticed. Elijah is lying on the earth, in the space between two timbers that support the planks."

"That sounds uncomfortable."

"It is. He can't sit up. But Nick and I have no safer place to hide him."

"I just returned from Niagara," said Hope. "I found Pa, but he doesn't believe I'm his daughter. He says my mother must have been unfaithful." Hope's voice faltered. "I came here because I couldn't think where else to go."

"What? Your mother unfaithful! Never!"

"Please. I can't bear to talk about it. I want to hear about Elijah. Where has he been? What brought him here?"

"He's been living with the Cherokees in Tennessee. Last summer he married a Cherokee girl. They're expecting their first child. He was talking so much about his mother and sister that finally his wife said, 'Go. Ease your mind. Return when you have seen them.' So he set out on his long journey. When he reached Kingston, he learned that his mother had died. That news made him even more determined to find you. His search led him to the orphanage. The orphanage sent him to a lawyer."

"Mr. McIsaac."

"Yes," said Charlotte. "And Mr. McIsaac told him that you'd gone to Niagara to look for your father. He explained that you had been indentured to Ephraim Block, who might be able to provide more information. He gave Elijah directions to reach Block's cabin. When Elijah arrived there, Ephraim wasn't home. He'd gone to Montreal."

"I know about this," said Hope. "I was present when Mr. McIsaac told Ephraim about British commissioners who'd be in Montreal to hear Loyalists' claims for compensation. I suppose Mr. McIsaac didn't realize that Ephraim had already left for Montreal."

"That sounds likely. When Elijah arrived at Block's place, he found Adam Anderson, the boy from the next farm, staying there to look after the dog and the chickens while Ephraim was away. Adam seemed happy to have a visitor. When he learned that Elijah was looking for you, they had a long conversation. In telling him about your letter to Colonel Butler, Adam mentioned Nick and me. As soon as Elijah heard that I lived in Milltown, he came here. He wanted to see me as an old friend, and because he hoped I could help him find you." Charlotte refilled their teacups. "The problem is, many men from Elijah's old regiment have settled around Milltown. They know he's a deserter. If he's recognized, his life is in danger. He thinks somebody may already have spotted him. When he told me this, I urged him to go back to Indian territory as fast as he could. But after coming all this way, he refuses to leave until he's seen you."

"I want to see him as much as he wants to see me," said Hope. Suddenly she was filled with excitement, a feeling so close to happiness that she could not help smiling. She forced her voice to stay soft and low. "I have an idea! There's an abandoned cabin on Ephraim's land, back in the woods. A hermit used to live there. Indians visit from time to time. Except for Ephraim and me, I don't think anybody else knows about it. I can take Elijah there. He'll be safe for a couple of days while we catch up on each other's life. Then he can go back to the Cherokees."

"I like your plan," Charlotte said thoughtfully. "It will be good for you and Elijah to spend time together. When I was a child, my three older brothers were the most important people in my life—apart from my parents. Like me, you had three older brothers, but you never knew them. That's very sad. Nothing can make up completely for what you missed, but this will help."

Hope nodded. "It will." She rubbed the sole of her shoe along the floor board, thinking that her brother could hear the scraping. It seemed a miracle that Elijah was only inches away. She wondered if he knew that she was here, and if he could hear any part of what was being said.

"You can go tonight," said Charlotte. "Most of the land between here and the Blocks' place is Clergy Reserve. The Church isn't required to clear its land. No farms. No roads. But Elijah has lived with the Cherokees long enough to know how to find his way through the forest in the dark. You can walk there in two hours."

A cry came from the cradle. Charlotte pushed back her chair. She said in a normal voice, "Joan needs feeding. After I've looked after her, it will be time to start dinner." She lowered her voice again. "Elijah must stay where he is until the children are asleep. Martha and Jack are too young to have any idea what's going on. As for Isaac, it's not that he couldn't keep a secret, but he would run all over town yelling, 'I've got a secret! I've got a secret! And I won't tell anybody what it is.'"

"He thinks he's a monkey," said Hope.

Charlotte laughed. "That's what I think, too."

CHAPTER 23

The Man beneath the Floor

THERE WAS A KNOCK at the door while Charlotte was tending to the baby.

"Come in!" she called.

The door opened and an old man entered, leaning on a crutch. He wore a red and black checked shirt and a red neckerchief. His white hair was tied at the nape of his neck. He was the same old man that Hope had seen through the window of the general store on her first visit to Milltown.

"I didn't know you had a visitor," he said. "I hope I'm not disturbing you."

"Of course not, Papa. This is Hope Cobman. I'm sure you

remember her." She paused, "Hope, I don't think you remember my father."

"I don't remember you, sir, but I've heard all about you," said Hope. "My mother told me how she hid you and Mrs. Hooper and Charlotte in her root cellar."

"Indeed she did," said Mr. Hooper. "That was a long time ago. My daughter has told me that you came to visit her in June. I'm pleased that this time I have a chance to greet you."

"Papa, would you like a cup of tea?" Charlotte asked.

"No thank you, daughter. I've just dropped by to ask if Jack and Martha would like to go for a walk."

The two children jumped up and ran to him shouting, "Yes! Yes!" Martha wrapped her arms around his knees.

"Not until they've put everything back in the toy box," said Charlotte. "That's the rule."

With Hope's help, that was quickly done. In a few minutes Charlotte and Hope were alone, except for baby Joan.

"Papa often takes them for a walk for half an hour after closing his store," said Charlotte. "It gives me a chance to catch my breath. I'm glad he came today. Without the children here, we can speak freely. 'Little pitchers have big ears,' as they say."

She brought the baby to Hope. "Would you like to hold her while I shell peas?"

"Glad to." Hope pushed back her chair from the table and reached out to take the baby, which nestled contentedly on her lap. "Joan looks like you," she said. "Same dark eyes."

"She's the only one who does," Charlotte said with a laugh. "The other three are blond like Nick."

Charlotte sat on a stool to shell the peas. "You know, Nick's taking a big risk by hiding Elijah. We're both taking a big risk. Every child in the school is the son or daughter of a discharged soldier. If the parents knew that the schoolmaster was hiding a deserter, there's no telling how many would take their children out of the school." Her busy hands stopped moving as she looked at her baby. "We'd be ruined."

Then she straightened her shoulders and snapped another crisp pod. "Nick wants to help Elijah. He understands how he feels. You see, Nick broke with his own family because of the war. His father called him a coward when he refused to join General Washington's army. Then he threw him out. They haven't seen each other since. Nick's father doesn't know he has four grandchildren. Maybe he wouldn't care. But it bothers Nick."

"Maybe he can go back for a visit and make peace with his father."

"He can't." Charlotte stood up and dumped the empty pods into the bucket under the dry sink. "First, he stole a horse to make his escape from a rebel recruiter. Then he went to work for the British, carrying dispatches. If Patriots caught him back in the Mohawk Valley, they'd put a noose around his neck."

Charlotte walked over to the fireplace and turned the crank to rotate the chicken roasting on the spit. "Thousands of families were broken apart like that. Have you heard of Benjamin Franklin?"

"I . . . think so." Hope felt embarrassed, as she so often did, by her own ignorance.

"A brilliant man, even though he was on the wrong side. He was a member of the Continental Congress. He invented the iron stove and all sorts of other things. His son William was Governor of New Jersey, a strong supporter of England. The break between them never healed. Benjamin Franklin died a few months ago without ever seeing his son again. That's tragic."

"It is." Hope thought about the gulf between her and her own father.

Charlotte beckoned Hope to come closer. Hope approached, carrying the baby. Charlotte whispered. "There's something I should tell you about Elijah. He's not well."

"What do you mean?" Hope felt a stab of fear. "Not consumption?"

"Nothing like that. It's because of everything he's been through." Charlotte kept her voice low. "I don't want to say more than that. Just be on your guard. Do nothing to cross him."

"I see." Hope remembered Ephraim telling her that there are wounds to the mind that the eye cannot see. "Damaged" was the word that Colonel Butler had used.

When supper was nearly ready and Mr. Hooper had brought back Martha and Jack, Charlotte picked up a cowbell from the mantel shelf. "I have to call Isaac," she said. She stepped outside onto the porch and rang vigorously. Hope thought the clanging could surely be heard a mile away.

A few minutes later Isaac arrived home, wet and muddy, with the announcement that he and his friends had been catching frogs down by the creek. Charlotte sent him to change into dry clothes.

Hope was setting the table when Nick came in. He looked at her with a puzzled expression, as if thinking, *Where have I seen you before?*

"This is Hope Cobman, Elijah's sister," said Charlotte.

His expression cleared. "Sorry I missed you when you visited last time. Charlotte told me that you're searching for your father."

"I found him. Our meeting did not go well. That's why I've come back here."

"I'm glad you did. Charlotte and I have been wondering how to get in touch with you." He pulled off his black, wide-brimmed hat—the kind of hat that farmers wore—and hung it on a hook inside the door. He was a tall, big-shouldered man who looked as if he belonged outdoors, although Hope remembered him as a pen-pusher on Carleton Island, organizing the transportation of Loyalist refugees to the mainland.

"Hope has a plan," said Charlotte. She gave Nick a sideways look that was packed with unspoken meaning. "I think it's exactly what we need. They're leaving tonight."

Nick nodded. "I see. I'm glad it will be tonight."

In a moment Isaac appeared in clean clothes. The plan was not mentioned again.

They all sat down at the wooden table to eat a delicious supper of warm biscuits, roasted chicken and fresh peas. For dessert there was apple cobbler. Hope barely tasted the little that she managed to eat. She couldn't stop thinking about Elijah, her long-lost brother who was right beneath their feet while they ate.

Nick and Charlotte passed plates, helped the children cut up their food and calmly carried on a conversation about this and that.

"Before we were married," said Charlotte, "we took it for granted that Nick would be a farmer. He worked hard to clear and cultivate his land, but every spare minute his nose was in a book. He'd rig it up so he could read while he plowed. Unfortunately, he kept running into stumps."

Nick laughed. "Charlotte said my head was in the clouds."

"It certainly was," said Charlotte, "but my feet were on the ground. I'd thought for a long time that Nick knew enough to be a teacher, even though he hadn't been to college."

Before now, the children had not said a word. Then Isaac piped up. "I'm going to be a soldier."

Nick looked at his son. "Really?"

Charlotte spoke firmly. "Isaac, it's not polite to interrupt while others are speaking."

Isaac ducked his head and took another spoonful of apple cobbler.

Charlotte continued. "When I told Nick that he ought to be a teacher, he admitted that he'd been thinking the same thing. So after he figured out what he'd have to charge the pupils in order to support his family, we sold our farm and bought a town lot. My father helped Nick build the schoolhouse."

"I've been a schoolmaster for four years," said Nick. "I have twenty pupils, all ages from seven to fourteen."

"I've heard it's a fine school," said Hope. "Adam Anderson wanted to go to it, but he had to settle for Mrs. Canahan's Sylvan Seminary for the Young Ideal."

Nick started to laugh and then checked himself. "Mrs. Canahan does her best."

After supper, Charlotte got the children ready for bed. Their bedroom was just off the main room. While washing dishes, Hope overheard the story of the Three Little Pigs and the Big Bad Wolf, a tale accompanied by huffs and puffs, squeals and howls, and followed by a chorus of "Good nights."

Charlotte finally closed the bedroom door and returned to join the others at the table. Nick listened attentively while Hope described the abandoned cabin and Charlotte explained the plan. When they had finished, Nick said, "It sounds like the best solution we're likely to find."

At last all sounds from the children's bedroom ceased. "Let's get on with it," said Nick.

They rose from the table. Nick grasped one end of the table; Hope and Charlotte took the other. With the table lifted out of the way, two fresh cuts in the wooden floor were easily seen. The loose section of plank was six feet long and as wide as the trunk of the tree from which it came.

Hope held her breath while Nick pried up the loose plank. It felt as if he were opening a grave. When the plank was removed, the man lying on his back blinked and rubbed his eyes. He raised his arms for Nick to help him rise from his hiding place. After setting him on his feet, Nick kept his hand under his elbow to steady him.

There was a dazed expression on Elijah's face. His brown hair was matted and dirty. From the waist down, Hope might have taken him for an Indian; he wore beaded moccasins, buckskin leggings and a fringed pouch, and he had a tomahawk in his belt. Above his belt he sported a green and black checked shirt. But what he wore was unimportant. She saw blue eyes, a pug nose and jug ears just like hers.

"Hello, sister," he said. Shaking off Nick's hand, Elijah took two steps forward and gave her a hug. It felt stiff and awkward, a hug between strangers. Then he let her go. His eyes flicked nervously around the room. He glanced to the left and to the right, even though the curtains were closed to prevent anyone from seeing inside.

"Could you hear what we were talking about?" Charlotte asked.

"About the cabin in the woods? I heard most of it."

"I have blankets and food ready for you to take," said Charlotte, "but let's have tea before you go."

Elijah seemed not to hear.

Charlotte spoke again, "Elijah, would you like a cup of tea?"

He looked at her. "Tea? That's a good idea." He walked around to the far side of the table and sat down facing the door. By the time they finished the tea, it was fully dark outside.

"It's safe to leave now," Nick said.

Elijah shook his head. "The fire casts enough light for someone to see us go out the door."

He refused to budge until the fire in the fireplace had burned to embers. The mantel clock struck ten before Hope and Elijah emerged from the dark house into the dark night.

CHAPTER 24

A Change of Plan

THEY CAME TO THE derelict cabin in the middle of the night, bringing with them two rolled-up blankets that Elijah carried across his shoulders and the food that Charlotte had packed.

The cabin had no door. There were gaps between the logs, and the moon was bright through the holes in the roof. Elijah let Hope have both blankets, one to lie on and one as a cover. He sat down on the dirt floor, leaning against the back wall and facing the empty door frame.

"Why don't you lie down?" Hope asked.

"I've been lying down enough to last a week."

"Can you sleep sitting up?"

"I can't sleep anyway."

He was still sitting there staring into the night when she rolled onto her side and fell asleep.

When Hope awoke in the morning, she heard him moving about outside. She rose and looked out through the empty doorway. Elijah had washed his shirt and was spreading it on a bush to dry. Seeing him stripped to the waist, she noticed that he wore a tiny leather bag suspended by a thong around his neck. It was covered with mysterious signs. The bag was something an Indian would wear.

They sat down to eat bread and cheese. Only a few feet away, a robin was splashing about in the little creek that ran by the cabin. The water sparkled in the morning sunshine, and the woods were filled with birdsong.

"It's a beautiful day," said Hope.

"Is it?"

"Don't you think so?"

"What's the difference?"

Now what should she say? She had waited such a long time to see Elijah. They had so much catching up to do, yet she didn't know how to talk to him. They were strangers. Except for having the same father and mother, there was nothing in either of their lives that they shared.

He ate silently, only his jaw moving, staring straight ahead. Surely there was some way to break the silence.

"When I saw you before," she said, "I was just a little thing, living in the barracks with Ma. It's one of my earliest memories. You took me onto your knee and gave me a piece of molasses candy. You wore a red coat with white cross belts. I found it hard to believe you were my brother. You were so grown up! Ma said I had two more brothers besides you. But you were the only one who ever came to see me. I never saw my father, either, until a few days ago."

"I know about that," said Elijah. "I overheard part of what you told Charlotte. You went to Niagara, and Pa said you weren't his child. But he's wrong."

"That's what I tried to tell him."

"What you told him is what Ma told you. He doesn't know it's the truth, but I do. I was there in the months before you were born. I saw for myself. He'd have to listen to me."

Hope kept silent. Charlotte had warned her not to cross Elijah. Did that mean she had to agree with everything he said?

A crumb of bread had dropped onto the grass. An ant, having found it, was struggling to drag it away. The crumb was twice the size of the tiny insect. Hope wondered how far it would go before giving up.

Elijah said, "When I set out from Chickamauga, I didn't plan to look for Pa and Silas. Just for you and Ma."

"Why not Pa and Silas?"

"Being soldiers, they were sure to know about me . . . that I'd deserted. Pa would reject me faster than he rejected you."

"Oh, no! I'm sure he would understand."

Elijah shook his head. "He'd say I'm a disgrace to my regiment. That's how soldiers think."

"I can't believe Pa would feel that way. But it doesn't matter. Even if you wanted to see him, it would be dangerous for you to go to Niagara. There are hundreds of soldiers at Fort Niagara and Navy Hall. You'd surely be recognized. What you need to do now is go back to the Cherokees as fast as you can. You know about Ma. You've seen me. That's what you came for."

"I'm changing my plan." As he spoke he stared straight ahead, not looking at her.

"You mean you aren't going back? Oh, you must! You can't leave your wife . . . and your baby!"

"Stop! You don't understand. If that were what I meant, I wouldn't be the first white man to abandon his native family. But that's not it. I certainly will return to Chickamauga. But first, you and I are going to Niagara. I'm not giving up until Pa accepts you as his daughter."

"No, Elijah. Leave Pa alone. He's sick. I don't mean in his head—at least not just in his head. He has the same cough Ma had before she died."

"Are you sure?"

"I was with Ma right to her last day. I know what consumption looks like and sounds like."

Elijah did not speak for a long time, and then he said, "All the more reason to go. Listen to me. As a sergeant in a Loyalist regiment, Pa received a land grant of two hundred acres.

When he dies, you have every right to inherit his land. But you won't get it unless he acknowledges you as his child."

She laughed nervously. "Whatever would I do with two hundred acres of trees, mosquitoes and wild animals?"

"You could sell the land if you didn't want it. Let's not worry about that. You and I are going to Niagara." He paused. "He's my father, too. I want to see him before he dies. Despite everything, he may want to see me."

The ant was still dragging the crumb. It had moved its prize a good ten inches from where it began and didn't look ready to give up.

"Then I suppose we must go." Hope sighed. "How will we get there? I don't have enough money to pay two fares on the packet boat. Even if I did, it wouldn't be safe. Whatever we do, you must not be recognized."

"We'll walk. I've travelled longer trails than that."

"It's two hundred miles."

"That's not very far."

"Don't you want to be back in Chickamauga before your baby is born?"

"My wife sent me on this mission. She wouldn't want me to return before I felt it was complete. She's in good hands with her mother and sisters. But if we start right now, I can still reach home before the birth. It's early September and the baby won't be born until November—Freezing Moon, we call it."

"Do we just start walking?"

"Why not?"

"All we have to eat are two apples and some bread and cheese."

"I'll set snares. I'll catch fish. We can gather nuts."

He was clenching and unclenching his fists. Charlotte had warned Hope not to cross him. And if she went with him, maybe he could persuade their father to accept her as his child. She didn't give a fig about the two hundred acres, but to hear him call her his daughter would be worth the two-hundred-mile walk.

"Very well," Hope said. "I'll come with you. But there's one thing I want to do first. I want to fetch my dog."

"What dog?"

"His name is Captain. You must have seen him when you were talking to Adam."

"You mean that big black and white puppy with the yellow eyes? Of course I remember him. I just didn't know he was your dog."

"That's him. I left him there when I went to Niagara, but I can take him back any time I want."

"He's half wolf, isn't he?"

"Yes. And the other half is sheep dog."

"That mix should make a good guard dog. All right. Get him. While I wait for you, I'll scout around for a back-country trail through the bush. There's too much settlement along the shoreline. The fewer people who see me, the less chance I'll be caught."

She set off on the path. As well as reclaiming her dog, Hope had a bit of unfinished business to attend to. She wanted to make peace with Adam. How fortunate that Ephraim had left Adam in charge of the cabin, giving her a chance to see him again! Their parting had been awkward. She had hurt his feelings. She owed him an apology.

She stopped walking, thinking what else was involved. Did she also owe him a kiss? Kissing the cow had not bothered her. Kissing a boy was a more serious matter. On thinking it over, she decided that she would like to kiss Adam. Having never kissed a boy, she was not sure how to go about it. Hope started walking again. By the time she reached the end of the path and emerged from the woods, she was wondering whether his big nose would get in the way.

Then she saw the clothesline. It had not been there a month ago. But there it was, a rope strung from one tree to another. On it hung a blue calico gown, a white petticoat and two pairs of striped stockings.

Hope stopped, unsure what to do next. She was standing there staring at the garments on the clothesline when the cabin door opened and a young woman stepped outside onto the doorstep. She was slim and pretty. On her head was a ruffled cap that did not hide all of her golden curls.

"Oh!" the young woman exclaimed. She whirled around, turned back into the cabin and shut the door.

CHAPTER 25

The Unexpected

HOPE WAS STANDING THERE wondering what was going on when the door opened again. This time it was Ephraim who came out, followed by Captain. Ephraim stopped cold. But as soon as Captain saw Hope, he raced to her, wagging his tail.

While Ephraim and Hope stared at each other, Captain jumped up and down, desperate to capture her attention.

"What are you doing here?" Ephraim asked.

She glanced from Ephraim to the cabin and back again. "I could ask you the same question. I thought you were in Montreal and Adam was staying here."

"Adam's gone home. We returned yesterday."

"We?"

"My wife Philippa and I. I gather you've met her."

"Not exactly met."

"I found her in Montreal and brought her back."

So the gossip had been true. Adam's mother had the story more or less straight. What had happened in Montreal? How had Ephraim found his wife? Those were interesting questions, but too personal to ask.

"That's good. I mean, it's good you found her." Hope couldn't think what else to say. Captain butted his head against Hope's leg, still trying to be noticed. She reached out and patted his head. He licked her hand.

"See," said Ephraim, "Captain didn't forget you. I suppose you've come to take him away."

"I hope you don't mind."

"Not at all. That was our understanding." He gave a nervous laugh. "Besides, I no longer need a dog for company."

Hope glanced toward the cabin. She saw a quick movement at the window. Philippa must be watching.

"Why did she run back into the cabin when she saw me?" Hope asked.

"Embarrassment. Panic. Philippa has been through a terrible time. I suppose you've heard the story? From the way people looked at me and said nothing, I figured everyone knew that my wife had run away."

"I did hear about her," Hope admitted.

"Her relatives in Philadelphia turned their backs on her

when they learned of her disgrace. I didn't know that she had been abandoned in Montreal. She was working for a laundress who paid her two shillings a week. I was taking my frock coat to be pressed, and there she was, standing at an ironing board pressing a gentleman's cravat. When she saw me, she stood rooted to the spot, her hot iron resting on the cravat. We stared at each other. The smell of scorching brought the laundress running. I paid for the cravat and took Philippa away.

"I won my case for compensation. Now Philippa and I are going to make a fresh start. She's forgiven me for not looking after her better." A dark look passed over Ephraim's face. "As you know, my mother could be very demanding."

"That's true."

"Now what about you? When I saw you last, you were on your way to Niagara. What happened there?"

"I talked with Colonel Butler. I visited my father. Now I'm going back to Niagara . . . with my dog." Hope was flustered. She was not lying, yet these half-truths felt like lies. She suspected that they sounded like lies.

Nothing in Ephraim's expression changed. "It sounds like a lot of travel, coming back here just to fetch your dog."

Hope had already said as much as she wanted to say. She had no desire to admit that her father had rejected her. Nor would she divulge to Ephraim or to anyone else that the Milltown schoolmaster had been hiding a deserter. Remembering Ephraim's sympathy for Elijah, she was tempted to tell him that she had found her brother, but she did not dare.

Ephraim broke the silence. "I must get back to Philippa. She's not strong. I mean, physically she's strong, but not in some other ways."

"I'm happy you found Philippa." Hope spoke what she truly felt. "Happy for her. Happy for you. You know what people say, 'All's well that ends well.'"

Ephraim gave a quiet smile. "You are indeed a wise girl."

He reached down to scratch Captain's ear. The dog was now sitting on his haunches, panting, his tongue hanging out. "When he gains some sense, this will be a fine dog," said Ephraim. "I'll miss him. But I'm sure that Adam will save another one for me."

"Is Woeful pregnant again?"

"Woeful is usually pregnant, according to Adam. He tells me that their neighbour on the other side has a hound that's been sniffing around. He expects that the next litter will be half hound. Good hunting dogs. That's really what I need." He gave a slight bow, turned toward the cabin, and at the door he waved goodbye.

"C'mon Captain!" said Hope. "We have a long way to go."

When they returned to the Squire's cabin, Hope did not see Elijah anywhere about. It was not until Captain bounded inside that Hope realized her brother was there. He was sitting against the back wall with tears streaming down his cheeks.

He looked up. His shirt had dried, and he was wearing it again. He wiped his eyes with the sleeve.

"Elijah, what's wrong?" she asked.

In an instant his expression changed to one of anger. He leapt to his feet. "Why did you come sneaking up on me?"

She recoiled. "But . . . but . . . I didn't!"

He raised his fist. "Don't. You. Ever. Do. That. Again."

Was this her brother, who had been so friendly when she left him an hour ago? Weeping. Raging. And now she was to travel with him on a long journey through the wilderness.

Captain placed himself between Hope's legs and peered out from under her skirt. He whimpered.

CHAPTER 26

On the Trail

ELIJAH LED THE WAY. Hope followed. Captain roamed about
everywhere. On the path. Off the path. Ahead of them. Behind them. He was clearly enjoying this adventure.

For Elijah it was not an adventure. He was constantly looking around. He started at every caw of a crow. The pace was
too fast for Hope, forcing her to strain to keep up. She wished
she could ask him to walk more slowly, but she did not want
to risk another outburst.

It was midday when a sharp pain finally forced her to cry
out, "Elijah, I need to stop!" He whirled about as if her words
were an attack. One hand went to the tomahawk at his belt.

She flinched at his sudden motion. "I have a stitch in my side from walking too fast."

He shook his head as if waking up. "What! Why didn't you tell me?"

"You seemed in such a hurry," she gasped, clutching her side.

"We are in a hurry. I want to get to Niagara in seven days."

"Two hundred miles in seven days?"

"A warrior in good condition can do that."

"But I'm not a warrior in good condition." She eased herself to the ground under a big maple tree and leaned back against its trunk. Captain trotted to her, cocked his head and stared questioningly. "Don't worry, Captain," Hope said, "I'll be fine." She took deep slow breaths until the pain eased.

Elijah looked over his left shoulder and then over his right before sitting down, also against a tree. He never, she noticed, left his back exposed.

Assured that Hope needed no further attention, Captain was sniffing in the long grass beside the trail. He made a stiff-legged jump. Something squeaked. Captain lifted his head. The long tail of the small creature between his jaws hung limply. He cocked his head, looking surprised at his success.

Elijah gave a short laugh, "Maybe he can catch something for you and me. We must be nearly out of food."

"We have two apples left." She took them from the satchel that Charlotte had packed. They were juicy, crisp delicious apples from the tree in her front yard. Hope began to feel better.

Elijah chewed steadily, not speaking until his was half finished. Finally he said, "I was worse before. What you saw back
at that cabin was a weak echo of the rages I used to have. A
bad memory would strike me, and I'd explode. At night I
couldn't sleep. It was so bad I wanted to end my life. That's
how sick I was when the Cherokees took me in. They held a
healing ceremony. Masks, dancing, drumming, prayers . . . It
helped. Now Swims Deep takes good care of me."

"Swims Deep?"

"My wife."

Hope thought Swims Deep was a strange name. She asked
simply, "What's she like?"

"Wise. Very kind. We live in a log cabin that her father and
brothers helped me to build."

"Ma kept me away from the Mohawk camp outside the
fort on Carleton Island," said Hope. "I can't imagine what living with Indians would be like."

"In some ways it's different, but not in others."

"But what is it like? Tell me about the village where you
live."

"I'm not good at describing things. Some families have
built log cabins, like white settlers. Others live in lodges that
have a framework of poles covered with bark slabs. There's a
council house where we hold meetings and ceremonies and
festivals. Lots of festivals. Cherokees have a big get-together
to celebrate almost everything. They're very sociable."

"I thought all Indians were fierce and warlike."

"Is that what Ma told you?"

"She said their souls were black as pitch, though she did allow there might be two or three good ones. She admitted that we owed our lives to the Mohawks who took us in their canoe to Carleton Island."

"Yes. They saved our lives." Elijah threw his apple core into the bushes. "It's likely that you'll meet one of those same Mohawks before today is over."

She looked around. "Where? On this trail?"

"We'll stop at their village on the Bay of Quinte. It's called Tyendinaga. I have a friend living there. His name is Okwaho. It means Wolf. He was my hero when I was thirteen. Okwaho was eighteen. He taught me to hunt with the bow and arrow." Elijah smiled. "Those were the best days of my life. When the Mohawks had delivered us safely to the fort on Carleton Island, I begged Okwaho to take me with him on his travels. He refused. But he called me his brother and gave me a medicine bag."

"A what?"

Elijah slipped one hand inside his shirt and pulled out the tiny leather bag that Hope had seen him wearing when they were at the Squire's cabin.

"You carry medicines in *that*?" She imagined pills, salves, syrups and tinctures.

"Medicine doesn't always mean the same thing. Okwaho told me that this bag contains a stone the colour of blood and a dust made from the skin of a rattlesnake and the beak of an eagle. Okwaho said that as long as I didn't open the bag, the medicine would make me a good hunter and strong warrior." He gave a bitter laugh. "Not strong enough, as it turned out."

He tucked the medicine bag back inside his shirt. "I haven't seen Okwaho since the day he gave me the medicine bag. I never expected to see him again. But Charlotte told me where he and his wife are living. Our trail runs through that land." He stood up. "We'll be there before sunset if you can walk another ten miles."

Hope was not sure that she could, but the stitch in her side was gone. She stood up cautiously. There were more questions that she wanted to ask, but Elijah seemed to have run out of words. Talking about Okwaho had brought him to life, but after that outpouring of enthusiasm, he sank into silence again.

CHAPTER 27

Tyendinaga

TYENDINAGA WAS NOT LIKE any town that Hope had seen before, with streets and shops. Here there were log cabins that appeared to have been set down randomly, scattered about in no special way. Roughly in the centre stood a long, low building where something seemed to be happening.

A crowd had gathered. People were seated on blankets in the open air, men on one side and women on the other, in a semi-circle. All were looking at the warrior who stood outside the building's entrance, holding an eagle feather in his hand. He was a man of middle age and middle height. His head had been shaved, except for his scalp lock, which was covered with a decoration made up of feathers, fur and beads.

"What's happening?" Hope asked. "Is it a festival?"

"No. It seems to be something serious. The warrior holding the feather is making a speech. He's John Deserontyon, their chief."

Elijah led her close enough for them to hear what was going on but not close enough to attract attention. Although Hope did not know what the chief was saying, she heard the passion in his voice. From time to time people nodded, murmuring their approval.

"What's he talking about?" Hope asked.

"I don't know the Mohawk language, except for a few words Okwaho taught me. But I did catch a name I recognize. Thayendanegea. That's Joseph Brant."

"The chief sounds angry," said Hope. She stood in silence, wondering whether he was inciting the Mohawks to go on the warpath. She remembered her mother's stories about Indian uprisings and slaughtered settlers.

Hope looked anxiously at her brother. "Maybe we should leave before anybody notices us."

"Shh!" Elijah's expression bore no sign of alarm. He was not even looking at the speaker but was studying the faces of the warriors who sat listening, his eyes moving from one to another.

Suddenly he whispered, "There's Okwaho."

"Which one?"

"The one with the feather on his cap." The warrior Elijah

was pointing to had bold cheekbones and a hawk's beak of a nose. His cap was shaped like a dome, from the top of which rose a single feather. Around the base of the quill, bands of small feathers were sewn to the cap. His eyes were on the speaker.

When Deserontyon finished his speech and set down the eagle feather, people rose from the blankets where they had been sitting and broke into little groups, talking earnestly.

"Are you going to speak to Okwaho?" Hope asked.

"Yes. Come along."

As they approached, Okwaho turned his head toward them, as if he suddenly realized that he was being watched. His eyes were dark, observant, intense. As he fixed his gaze on Elijah, his brows knit in a frown.

Elijah raised his hand to shoulder height and took two steps forward. "Okwaho!"

"Ho!" The warrior returned the salute.

"I'm Elijah Cobman."

Okwaho's frown vanished. After a few words to his companions, he walked straight to Elijah. "I remember you. You're the boy who worked so hard to learn to hunt with the bow and arrow. You're taller now, and you've added some muscle."

"I've had plenty of time to finish growing," said Elijah. "The time you speak of was many years ago."

"I never thought I'd see you again," said Okwaho. He glanced at Hope. "Who is this?"

"My sister Hope."

"She was a newborn baby last time I saw her. You're right. That was many winters ago. What brings you to our village now?"

"Hope and I are on our way to Niagara to see our father. It happens that our trail runs through your lands."

"I am glad that you have stopped to visit us." He took Elijah's arm. "Come to my home. My wife will give us something to eat."

As they followed Okwaho, the yellow Indian dogs eyed Captain suspiciously, for his black and white coat made him distinctly different from them. They sniffed him, and one gave a tentative growl. Captain wagged his tail and showed no inclination to run or to fight. Not yet five months old, he was about as large as the Indian dogs, but he still had that puppy gawkiness that showed he was no threat.

Okwaho took Elijah and Hope to his log cabin, which had no furniture and no floor. Storage baskets and piles of furs lay against one wall. Okwaho placed beaver pelts on the ground for them to sit upon.

Okwaho's wife, whom he introduced as Drooping Flower, brought them bowls of fish and chunks of soft, moist cornbread. She was a tall, beautiful woman wearing a deerskin tunic over red cotton trousers. After bringing the food, she left Okwaho and his guests to eat undisturbed.

"What's going on?" was Elijah's first question. "I heard Thayendanegea's name."

"I'll explain the situation," said Okwaho. "We built this

village on the original tract of land on the Bay of Quinte that the British gave us to compensate for our lost home in the Mohawk Valley. As well as land, the British promised us a church, a school, a mill and tools for farming. Most of us were satisfied with this.

"But not Thayendanegea. He wanted to be closer to the Six Nations people who live in the United States. So he persuaded Governor Haldimand to arrange for the additional grant of a great tract of land, six miles on each side of the Grand River for its entire length. The church, school, mill and tools that were supposed to be for our village all went to the Grand River. When that happened, about four hundred Mohawks left Tyendinaga and moved there."

"How many stayed here?" asked Elijah.

"About one hundred. Thayendanegea wants the rest of us to leave the Bay of Quinte to join the others. But Chief Deserontyon is determined to stay here."

"Why doesn't he want to join the others?"

"Here, he's the chief. If we move to the Grand River, Thayendanegea will be the one in charge. Deserontyon doesn't like that idea. Thayendanegea has offered generous gifts. That's what the meeting today was about. Deserontyon was urging us to resist Brant's smooth talk and bribes. He reminded us that we've started our own school and we're building our own church. The Reverend John Stuart comes from Kingston to conduct church services. There's nothing we need that we don't have here."

This reluctance to move made perfect sense to Hope. Why should these people want to be uprooted a second time?

"But I've talked enough about us," Okwaho said to Elijah. "I want to hear about you. Where has the path of your life taken you? Are you a man of peace or a man of war?"

Hope lowered her face and inspected the toes of her shoes. What would Elijah say? How much of his story would he tell?

"I was in the army," Elijah answered. "The King's Royal Regiment of New York."

"Did you fight many battles?"

"More than I can count."

"How many enemies did you kill?"

Elijah's face hardened, becoming as rigid as a block of wood. "Sixteen."

"Sixteen! That makes you a great warrior. What's your favourite weapon? Sword? Musket? Bayonet?"

"Rifle. I was what they call a sharpshooter." Hope heard a quaver in his voice.

"That doesn't surprise me. Remember how I taught you to use the bow?"

Elijah seemed to relax a little. "You tied a dead squirrel to a high branch of a pine tree and made me keep trying until my arrow pierced it through."

"That is so. I saw that you had a keen eye and with practice would develop a deadly aim."

"Too deadly," Elijah muttered, but Okwaho did not hear him.

"Soon after that," said Okwaho, "your little brother ran away."

"His name was Moses. He was carried off by Oneidas," said Elijah. "They adopted him."

"Around our council fires there is much talk about a warrior they call the White Oneida."

"That's my brother. The Oneidas gave him the name Broken Trail. He's the only famous person our family ever produced. He seems to travel everywhere, negotiating treaties, making speeches."

"The White Oneida works for Thayendanegea." Okwaho almost spat the words.

"I don't take sides," said Elijah. "None of this is my concern."

Okwaho nodded. "No politics, then."

It was growing dark. Drooping Flower returned to the cabin and spread bear pelts on the ground for everyone to sleep on. Captain curled up outside the door.

Hope had never before had a bear pelt as a bed. The thick, springy fur was comfortable, but too warm for a sticky, humid late summer night. She dozed off, but after a while was wakened by the sound of the door opening and closing. Unable to go back to sleep, she went outside.

There was Elijah sitting with his back against a poplar tree, its silvery leaves aflutter in the breeze. The moon was full. By its light she saw tears running down her brother's face. She approached and sat down at his side.

"Sixteen men," he mumbled through his tears. "I didn't see one of them as a fellow human being. They were targets. The crossing of their white cross belts was the bull's eye. When I hit the mark and saw blood bloom like a red rose, I was a hero. I notched the stock of my rifle for each kill. But my killing didn't stop at sixteen men. There was one more. He was not an enemy; he was my friend."

Elijah's shoulders heaved, and he buried his face in his hands.

CHAPTER 28

Ghosts

BY MORNING ELIJAH HAD pulled himself together. Nothing in his bearing revealed any trace of his distress during the night. After taking their leave of Okwaho and Drooping Flower, Hope and Elijah returned to the trail. Heading southwest, they travelled through a forest of oak, maple and pine. Captain lagged behind, unwilling to let any hole in the ground remain unexamined, but he was never out of sight for long.

The path was heavily overgrown. Hope had to watch out for roots that snaked across the path. Slender branches that Elijah pushed out of the way had a spiteful tendency to whip back and slap her face. She seldom looked up; instead, she kept her gaze mostly fixed on the ground so that what she saw were her own scuffed shoes trudging along.

At sundown they stopped beside a narrow stream. Hope sank wearily onto the grass. "Why don't you sit down?" she asked Elijah. "Don't you ever get tired?"

"I've been tired for so long that I don't think about it." He opened the satchel, took out bread and cheese, and brought her share to her. "Eat this. It's all that's left of the food Charlotte packed. I'll set snares tonight. If I catch anything, we'll have food for tomorrow."

What if you don't catch anything? Hope kept her doubts to herself, fearful that a careless word would provoke another upset. She had always thought of a big brother as someone to look after her. Now she had found one of her big brothers, but he had problems worse than hers. At best, they might take care of each other. Maybe that wasn't a bad idea.

After looking to left and right, Elijah sat down with his back against a tree. "I wish there were some shelter," he said, "I don't like being in the open. Even though it was uncomfortable lying under the floor at Nick and Charlotte's home, I felt safe."

"It would have terrified me to be trapped with a plank over my head," said Hope. "If the person I was hiding from lifted the plank and saw me . . ." She shuddered.

"I almost hoped that would happen," said Elijah, "because then there would be nothing I could do. No way to escape. It would be a relief to have everything end."

"You don't mean that," Hope said. "If you really did, you wouldn't be here."

"I suppose that's true." After a long pause, he added, "Do you want me to light a fire?"

"Is it safe?"

"A campfire attracts attention if there's anyone about. On the other hand, it keeps wild animals away."

She thought about this. They had not met any other travellers on this old trail. As for wild animals, so far she had seen nothing bigger than a porcupine. But who knew what lurked in the forest at night?

"Do you want a fire, or not? Make up your mind." He was clenching his fists, his hands white at the knuckles.

She saw that he was fighting to control himself. But what had she said to upset him? Hope took a deep breath. "Yes. Please make a fire."

"Fine." He stood up. "You gather the firewood while I set snares." He walked off into the bush.

Hope was torn between relief at having him out of her sight, fear at being alone and anxiety about the kind of mood he would be in when he returned.

It was dusk when he came back. He seemed satisfied with the pile of dry twigs and branches that she had gathered. He took his flint, steel and tinder from his pouch. When he had a tiny flame going, he fed it the smallest twigs first, soon building up a healthy blaze.

Hope felt safe in the circle of firelight. Frogs croaked.

Crickets chirped. These were reassuring noises. Then in the distance a wolf howled. Captain jumped up, threw back his head and howled in return.

"Stop that noise!" said Hope. Captain looked sheepish and lay down again. "He doesn't know whether he's a dog or a wolf," she explained.

"That's something he'll have to figure out for himself," said Elijah. "I reckon it's a problem we all have, discovering what we are and not what others expect us to be." He seemed to be looking past her as he spoke, not seeing her at all.

She thought about what he had said. It made sense. Charlotte and Nick came to mind. Everybody had expected Nick to be a farmer. He too had taken it for granted. He looked like a farmer—a big man who seemed made for the outdoor life. But he and Charlotte had figured out that he was meant to be a teacher. *What about Elijah?* She asked herself. *What is he meant to be? What about me?*

Hope watched the flames sink to embers. She felt safe, with her blanket wrapped around her and Captain curled up against her back. The moon, which was just past the full, gave enough light for her to see Elijah resting against the tree. She wished he would lie down to get a proper rest. His wakefulness troubled her but was reassuring at the same time. It was like having a sentry on guard.

Hope was sound asleep when suddenly she was wakened by a shriek. She bolted up and stared about. So did Captain, his ears pricked and his nose pointed toward a frenzy of thrashing and snarling in the undergrowth only a few feet away.

"A lynx caught something. Nothing for you to worry about," said Elijah. She saw that he had his tomahawk in his hand.

She scrunched down into her blanket and pressed her palms against her ears. This shut out most of the noise of tearing, grunting and chomping. It did not make her stop trembling. Their next visitor might be a bigger animal, perhaps a cougar looking for a meal.

After a time, when the lynx had finished devouring its prey and had left, the shaking of her body lessened. She began to relax, but she did not go back to sleep.

At first light she crawled from her blanket. There was still some firewood left. She placed an armful of dry sticks on the embers. As the flames spurted, her little spark of courage seemed to grow. She was still alive. Maybe there was only a slim chance that this quest would succeed. If it failed, she would not be any worse off. There was her brother asleep with his back against the tree. By the light of the fire he looked soiled and unshaven. The bristles stood out on his jaw. If she could carry on to the end, no matter what the outcome, simply being with her on this long trail might do him some good.

One of Elijah's snares supplied a rabbit for breakfast. Elijah skinned it so deftly it looked as if he were peeling off a stocking. Without its furry hide, the rabbit was no longer an animal. It was meat. Elijah dumped the entrails onto the ground a few feet away to let Captain enjoy a feast. Wagging his tail, he poked his hungry muzzle into the slippery mess.

Elijah cut the rabbit into pieces that they grilled on green sticks over the fire. Since there was more than enough for one meal, they saved the hindquarters. Elijah wrapped the meat in leaves and tucked it into the satchel.

Halfway through the morning they came upon the ruins of a native village. Nothing remained except charred poles covered with grapevines.

"Huron lived here a long time ago," said Elijah. "Today, this trail connects nothing to nothing, but it wasn't always this way. There were many Huron villages. If you poke around in the grass, you'll find remains of lodges."

"Where did the Huron go?"

"The Iroquois killed them off. From further back than anyone remembers, the Iroquois and the Huron were enemies. When Europeans arrived, the Huron allied themselves with the French and the Iroquois with the English. What they got from these alliances were better weapons to kill each other. After the Iroquois wiped out the Huron, almost nobody lived in these lands until the Mississaugas moved in. We may meet a few along the way."

"I've already met some Mississaugas," said Hope. "They came to the Blocks' cabin with brooms and baskets to trade for food. Mrs. Block told them to go away."

"Most people tell them to go away. White people figure

that after you've sold your land, you're obliged to leave it. From the Mississauga point of view, all they gave was permission to share. But with so much white settlement, there's little game left. It's become harder and harder for the Mississaugas to feed themselves. They have a hard life."

"Are they dangerous?"

"They aren't a warlike nation. Of course, anyone can be dangerous if he's hungry enough."

Hope felt a cold chill as she looked around at the grassy space where nobody lived any longer. "I don't like this place. It's full of ghosts."

"You can't escape from ghosts. They follow you everywhere."

They returned to the trail. As Hope plodded on, she peered into the shadows between the trees and imagined ghostly shapes.

CHAPTER 29

Against the Wall

JUST BEFORE SUNSET they made camp on the shore of a marshy inlet where flotillas of yellow pond lilies bloomed on the surface of the water. Elijah made Hope a bed of spruce boughs. Then he made one for himself. A good sign. If he was going to sleep lying down, he must be getting better.

That night she lay on her spruce-bough bed, and Elijah lay on his. Captain snuggled against Hope's back. She listened drowsily to the peeping and croaking of a mighty chorus of frogs. Everything seemed fine when she went to sleep.

Hope dreamed she was lying on her cot in the barracks and she heard someone crying. The sound woke her. Someone *was* crying. But she was not in the barracks, and the sobbing came from Elijah. Hope didn't know what to do about it.

If she woke him, would he rage against her? Or would he be grateful for rescue from his demons? She had heard that it was dangerous to waken a person from a nightmare, although she did not know why. She remembered what Ma used to do for bad dreams. It was worth a try. Wriggling out of her blanket, and thus dislodging Captain from his comfortable spot pressed against her back, she crawled to Elijah. Laying her hand on the top of his head, she gently stroked his hair. At her touch he gave a twitch; she kept on stroking.

His sobs ceased, and she hoped that he would now drift into quiet sleep, but instead he started mumbling, and it sounded as though the most unutterable anguish was wrenched from him in every broken phrase. "Malcolm . . . don't look at me like that . . ."

She leaned over, put her mouth to his ear. "Elijah, it's just a dream. Wake up!"

But he would not stop. "Shoulder arms . . . Aim . . . No! I can't . . ."

She felt a furry shoulder press against her. Captain had come to help. He licked Elijah's cheek, licked it again and again. With Hope stroking his hair and Captain licking his cheek, Elijah woke up.

"What's going on?" He sat bolt upright.

"You had a nightmare."

"Did I say anything?"

She hesitated. "There was somebody called Malcolm."

Elijah held his head in both hands. "Sergeant Malcolm." Now his words came in a rush. "We were together at the siege of Charleston. Children screaming. Houses burning. People starving. We were sharpshooters, did our killing at a distance. This was close up. Too close. He couldn't take it anymore. He deserted. I understood. They caught him and brought him back. I was picked for the firing squad."

"Elijah, you don't have to tell me." She laid her hand on his arm.

He shook off her hand. "There were six of us in a row. The sun had just risen when they brought him from the guard-house. They'd stripped the buttons from his uniform. His face was grey. Sweat rolled down his face. He was trembling so hard that his guards had to support him. He didn't strug-gle when they stood him against the wall. I reckon he'd been awake all night thinking about what was going to happen to him, and he'd made up his mind to die with dignity.

"We were going to shoot at him until he was dead. If the first volley didn't hit any vital organs, there'd be a second vol-ley. The guards turned him around so he was facing us, his back pressed against the wall. His eyes held no expression until he saw me. I'll never forget the look he gave me. Shock and ... pity."

"Pity?"

"Because he knew what I had to do. We'd shared our

thoughts. He knew that mine were the same as his. He'd acted on them. I hadn't. If it had been the other way around, I would have been the one against the wall."

She felt his body tremble as he spoke. "I see it day and night—the way the way he looked at me before they tied the blindfold around his eyes. I can't bear to think about his final minutes while he waited for our bullets to slam into him. Did it seem a long time or a short time? I hope it was short." Elijah clenched and unclenched his fists. "After it was over, I knew I'd rather lose my own life than ever again take another's."

Hope contemplated his words for some minutes. "So you deserted."

"Yes."

In the silence that followed, she could hear Colonel Butler's voice: "Terrible things happen in war." These words were better than any she could think of, and so she said them.

Elijah nodded. "There's no glory in it at all."

They did not talk any more but sat close together as night faded and the first streaks of light penetrated the trees.

Would Elijah ever be whole again? People said, "Time will heal." Did it? Many years had passed. Surely by now time had done everything it could! The Cherokees had helped him with their healing ceremony. His wife Swims Deep had helped him with her loving care. Now it was up to her. What could she do to help him the rest of the way?

CHAPTER 30

The Test

THE SUN SHONE, birds sang, cicadas thrummed. This was Hope and Elijah's fourth day on the trail, and during that time they had not seen another human being.

Then three warriors stepped out from the trees. One moment the warriors were not there, and the next moment they were. Their faces were dark and angry. They wore leggings and breech cloth. No shirts. No scalp locks. Their hair was braided. Mississaugas. They blocked the path. One held a tomahawk, one a war club and one a bow with the arrow notched but the bowstring not pulled back.

Everything stopped. The forest was plunged into silence. Even the cicadas ceased their strident hum. Elijah stood as motionless as if he had been carved from wood. Hope wanted to scream but could not make a sound.

"Come with us," said the warrior holding the bow. He raised it, pointing the arrow at Elijah's throat, and drew the string halfway. Elijah did not move.

The metal arrowhead caught a flash of sunlight. Hope pulled her eyes away from the shiny tip. She did not want to see the arrow fly. The warrior with the tomahawk said something in his own language. She understood the menace in his voice.

The bowman pulled back the string even further and made a gesture with his head, indicating that Elijah should walk ahead, down the path. Elijah did not move. He seemed to be in a trance.

Where was Captain? Off chasing a squirrel, probably. If they ever needed a guard dog, it was now. Then from the corner of her eye Hope saw him bounding along the trail, catching up in his usual manner.

The warrior with the club saw him and raised the club. Captain woofed, wagged his tail and kept on coming. Puppy-like, he seemed to think this was a game. The warrior slung his club just as Captain jumped up. It was a wild swing, leaving the man's feet unbalanced. He stepped back, and at that instant fifty pounds of fur and muscle collided with his stomach and knocked him over. Suddenly, the warrior was on his back with the big, excited puppy standing on his chest. His war club lay at Hope's feet.

Hope's scream split the air. The bowman swung his bow

around, the string taut and the arrow aimed at her. He was ready to release it when Elijah came to life. With a shout, he sprang forward and knocked the bow aside. The arrow flew harmlessly into the trees.

Then Elijah laid about him with hands and feet. He caught the bowman by his braided hair, dragged his head back and forced him to the ground. Elijah was straddling the now bowless bowman when the warrior with the tomahawk charged. His tomahawk lifted high, he was ready to bring it down on the back of Elijah's neck.

What happened next was like a dream. Hope seemed to be watching as if it were another person who scooped up the fallen war club, clutched it in both hands and swung it hard. She felt the impact; it flew like lightning up both arms as the club struck the warrior's head. There was a sharp crack. He pitched forward, his face hitting the ground. Hope looked from the war club in her hands to the motionless figure on the ground. Had she really done that?

Captain, wildly barking, standing on the chest of the warrior he had knocked down, still seemed to think that this was a game. But then the warrior grabbed him by the throat to wrestle him aside. Captain squealed.

"Let go of my dog!" Hope shouted as she leapt, brandishing the war club. The warrior sank back, one hand releasing his grip on Captain's throat as he raised his arm to protect himself from the coming blow.

The threat was enough. Hope did not need to strike. The fight was over as quickly as it had begun.

Elijah's man was face down, one arm twisted behind his back while Elijah pulled a ball of cord from his pouch. Soon he had the warrior's wrists bound, and then his ankles. When that was done, he tied up the warrior whom Hope and Captain had overcome.

The third warrior, the one she had struck down, lay completely still, a trickle of blood running from his ear. Hope feared that she had killed him until she heard him groan.

The bowman's quiver and bow were lying on the ground. Elijah pulled an arrow from the quiver, inspected it and then set it down. Next he tried the bow, pulling back the string to test the tension. He was smiling. This was the first time Hope had seen him smile.

"Hope," he said, "roll this fellow onto his back. I want him to see what I can do with his bow."

Hope obeyed. The warrior stared up at Elijah. As he watched Elijah fit an arrow to the bowstring, he began to sing. His song was not like any music Hope had heard before. It was a chant intoned on the same two or three notes, a monotonous, doleful droning sound. Then the warrior whom Captain and Hope had defeated began to sing the same way.

"Stop that din," Elijah ordered. "Save your death songs for another day."

The bow's former owner stopped singing. The other, who apparently did not understand English, kept on until he too realized that Elijah had no intention of killing them.

As soon as they were quiet, Elijah notched the arrow. "Watch this," he said. "See that squirrel?" With one swift, sure motion he raised the bow, aimed, pulled back the bowstring and let the arrow fly.

The doomed squirrel was sitting high in an oak tree eating an acorn when its life came to a sudden end.

"I never before saw a white man who could shoot like that," said the warrior after the dead squirrel dropped, its body neatly skewered. He turned to look at Hope, "or any girl who could handle a war club."

Hope felt like laughing. A sense of triumph filled her. She had never before felt so alive.

"Why did you want to capture us?" Elijah asked.

"We planned to hold you hostage. White people pay much money to get you back."

"You picked the wrong quarry. Nobody would pay a shilling for either of us."

Elijah took possession of the bow and quiver of arrows, the tomahawk and the club. He pulled the arrow from the body of the squirrel and put it in the quiver. He tossed the squirrel to Captain, who shook it vigorously to make sure it was dead. They left the three warriors where they lay, two tied up and one half-unconscious. Captain carried the squirrel in his mouth.

When they had walked some distance, Elijah threw the war club and the tomahawk into the bushes, but he kept the bow and quiver of arrows.

"The warriors we tied up will be able to free themselves," Elijah said, "but it will take them a while. The one you hit on the head won't be going anywhere for the rest of the day. The others will stay with him until he's feeling better."

"Aren't you afraid they'll get their friends and come after us?"

"No. We'll have too much of a head start. And besides, we've earned their respect. Especially you. I never before realized how brave you are."

"I was terrified. I screamed."

"Being brave doesn't mean you don't feel fear. It means doing what you have to do even when you're afraid."

"Captain was the real hero," said Hope. "The way he came bowling along the trail, knocked that man over and then stood on his chest." She glanced down at the dog. With the squirrel's tail dangling from one side of his mouth, he had more of a comic than a heroic look.

"I'll give him credit for taking that man down," said Elijah, "but I won't call him a hero. The protective instinct won't appear in him for another four or five months. For Captain, it was just a game."

Elijah laid his arm across Hope's shoulder. "You're the hero. You're the one who saved my life." She saw that his eyes were clear, and it seemed that the darkness had passed from them.

CHAPTER 31

What if...?

IF ELIJAH'S SICKNESS had been of the body, Hope would have said that the fever broke that day. Growing up in the Fort Haldimand barracks, where soldiers and refugees shared the same quarters and the same illnesses, she had seen plenty of sickness. Sometimes the sick person died, sometimes he or she recovered. There was always a crisis, a turning point.

She watched Elijah closely the next day and the next. He was quiet, silent for hours on end. Yet it did not seem to be a troubled silence. At night he slept soundly. Their meeting with the Mississaugas had turned out to be a double victory for Elijah. Finally, he had laid his ghosts to rest.

In Hope's eyes the journey was already a success, no matter what awaited them at Niagara. Even if Elijah failed to convince Pa that she was his child, she had found her brother, and her brother had found himself again. This was what she had wanted most, and now she had it.

Elijah made good use of the captured bow and arrows. Each evening they feasted on wild turkey, rabbit or grouse. Black walnuts were plentiful. Elijah said that it was the best of time of year for being on a long trail. Although he had given up the idea of reaching Niagara in seven days, they kept going at a steady pace.

The nights became chilly and the trees were changing colour. Overhead, the first skeins of wild geese were flying south in ragged arrowheads. On the ninth morning of their journey, Elijah pointed west and said, "Look that way. What do you see?"

"A cloud bank." She squinted. "Or is it a mountain?"

"Neither. It's an escarpment."

"What's an escarpment?"

"It's a kind of cliff where the land above it is higher than the land below it. The one we're looking at is hundreds of feet high and thousands of miles long. The Niagara River plunges over it; that's where all the water from Lake Erie pours into Lake Ontario."

"You mean Niagara Falls! Will we reach Butlersburg before long?"

"Not Butlersburg. I can't go there. This trail will end at the Niagara River halfway between Queenston and Butlersburg."

"That's not far from Pa's cabin."

"Then we'll be there tomorrow."

So this was to be their last full day on the trail. The thought made her melancholy, and it seemed that nature shared her feeling of gloom. As the day went on, the sky clouded over. A light drizzle was falling by the time they stopped for the night.

Using his tomahawk as a hatchet, Elijah cut spruce boughs to make a canopy, and then he pinched off the tender tips to brew spruce tea. He claimed this tea to be a most healthful drink for keeping off chills. Although she found it sour to taste, Hope welcomed the warmth, for the mizzle of rain had chilled her through and through. They grilled the rabbit he had shot that day. After eating, Hope and Elijah sat companionably, each wrapped in a blanket, and watched the fire from under their canopy. The fire sizzled and popped as drop by drop the rain tried to put out the flames.

Like her, Elijah was quiet and thoughtful. "Whatever happens," he said, "I'm grateful for this journey. From now on, I'm going to live one day at a time and look no further back than yesterday."

It seemed to Hope that it was likely better for Elijah not to look back. But she had memories that she cherished, and even the bad times had taught her something. She said, "When I was growing up, I always liked hearing Ma talk about the old days in Canajoharie. Her stories made me wonder what our life would be like if the war had never happened."

"I can answer that question. We'd be living in Canajoharie. Pa and Silas would be working at the grist mill, because that was what they were doing before they joined Butler's Rangers. I'd be a master carpenter by now, because I'd had plans to be apprenticed to that trade."

"What about Moses?"

"Moses? I don't know. He hated school. He didn't like anyone telling him what to do. It's hard to say how he would have turned out."

"And me? What would I be doing if there hadn't been a war?"

"You're nearly fourteen, so you'd be done with school. If Ma were alive, you'd be helping her with the cooking and cleaning. She'd be teaching you to spin and weave and make quilts—all those things girls have to learn. You might have a sweetheart."

"Ma wouldn't have allowed that."

"Why not?"

"Sweethearts lead to marriage. She counted on me to stay single to look after her in her old age."

"Did she, now?" He looked at her oddly. "What did you think of that idea?"

"It worried me. Not that I was interested in boys. I didn't like them very much, not the ones in the barracks. But if I didn't get married, there would be no one to look after me. That was my greatest fear. Pa and my brothers going away and not coming back—that's what caused it."

"So you looked at a husband as somebody to take care of you. Do you still see it that way?"

"Not any longer. I think a woman should be able to take care of herself." As soon as this speech was out of her mouth, Hope remembered where she had heard almost those same words before. In her mind's eye she saw Mrs. Block sitting in her bentwood chair, proclaiming in her powerful voice that a woman should take pride in looking out for herself. Maybe she had learned something important—besides how to cook—from that old tyrant. "On the other hand," Hope added, "since then, I've met one or two boys I've liked. Perhaps I shall have a sweetheart someday."

"I think," said Elijah, and Hope heard a note of admiration in his voice, "that you are going to make your way in the world very well."

CHAPTER 32

Missing

HOPE OPENED HER EYES on the daylight. Through the dripping trees she could see clear blue sky. It would be a good day for walking.

They started out early. All day she and Elijah followed the bench of the escarpment. There were pretty waterfalls, some cascading over the brink, others springing from fissures in the rock face. The trail took them through woods of black walnut, maple and oak. In forest glades, wild grapevines draped themselves over sun-warmed boulders and green bushes.

They walked east and further east. Then the trail came to

an end. They had reached the wagon track that ran along the west bank of the Niagara River. Although empty now, it was a well-travelled road, rutted by wheels and pitted with hoof prints left by horses and oxen.

Elijah crossed the road and stood at the edge of the gorge. Hope hung back.

"Come see the view," he called to her.

She did not move. Even the idea of looking into the abyss produced a surge of fear. Ensign Dunn had called it vertigo: the dizzy feeling, the roaring in her ears and the terrifying urge to leap.

"I'll stay here. I'm afraid of heights."

He returned to her side. "Do you know where we are?"

She looked around. "I don't recognize any landmarks. We must be upriver from Pa's place. If we follow the river, we'll come to his cabin before long."

It was late in the day. Only one wagon came toward them as they walked. As soon as it was in view, they took cover on the side of the road further from the brink. The wagon driver did not notice them. He was an old man with a white beard, rounded shoulders and a broad-brimmed hat. He stared ahead, not looking to either side as his wagon bounced along. The horse and wagon also looked old, but the barrels with which the wagon was loaded were not. Their iron hoops were black and their staves had the creamy whiteness of new-sawn wood. The old man was probably trying to reach Queenston before dark.

Hope, Elijah and the dog remained hidden until the wagon was a safe distance further along the road. Then they started walking again.

The sun was setting when Hope halted. "Now I know where we are." She pointed to a well, enclosed by a dry stone wall, beside a path that ran north from the road. "That's where Pa has to go for water. His own well is bad. His land is just beyond."

In a few minutes they came to the path that ran from the road to Pa's cabin. "That's it," she said. The cabin looked just as shabby as it had when she saw it the first time. The path was even more overgrown.

Elijah scratched his head and frowned. "It doesn't look good."

He walked ahead of her to the cabin. His hand hovered at the door, knuckles ready to knock. Although his hesitation lasted only for a moment, it was long enough for Hope to realize that he was as nervous as she was.

Then he knocked. Hope listened for some sound on the other side of the door. A footstep. A creak. There was nothing. Elijah raised his fist and knocked again. No response.

"There's nobody here," said Hope. A chill came over her. She thought about the old Squire. *What if Pa . . . ?*

"I'll see." Elijah pressed the latch. The door opened. He stepped into the gloom. She stayed outside, listening to his footsteps on the plank floor. Captain looked up at her anxiously and gave a low whimper.

Elijah returned. "He's not here." At the relief in his voice, Hope realized that he too feared what he might find inside.

She entered, followed by the dog. The dust and cobwebs made the cabin look deserted, but the reek of dirty clothes, stale sweat and sickness told a different story. Captain walked about, sniffing everything. Elijah knelt at the fireplace and held his hand over the ashes.

"Still warm," he announced. "Pa's gone somewhere and not that long ago."

She looked around. The dirty dishes and the bed with its filthy blanket were just as before. But one thing was missing from the scene: the water bucket.

"He's gone for water," Hope said. "He keeps the bucket under the shelf. It's not there."

"If Pa went to that well we passed, we would have met him on the way."

"We would have," Hope agreed, "if . . . unless . . ."

Elijah stood up. "We'll track him. I know how to read a trail, and Captain can use his nose. He took the blanket from the bed. "Come here, Captain. Smell this."

Captain buried his muzzle in the folds, and then he looked up, bright eyed, instinctively grasping what was expected of him.

"He understands," said Elijah. "Let's go."

CHAPTER 33

No Other Way

THEY LEFT THE CABIN. Elijah paced back and forth, bent over, eyes examining the ground. Captain walked in circles, his nose searching for the scent.

Hope waited on the doorstep until Elijah called, "This way! I've found his tracks. He's headed toward the river." She pushed her way through vines and bushes to Elijah. He pointed to the ground. "See those footprints? He's staggering." All that Hope saw were scuffed and trampled leaves.

The trail turned right at the road, heading upriver. Although Pa had left no visible footprints on the wagon rack, Captain's nose had no trouble following the scent.

"He's going toward his neighbour's well," said Hope. But suddenly the trail veered off the road and toward the gorge that yawned ahead of them, no more than ten feet away.

"I see footprints in the grass," said Elijah. "He's weaving. His steps are uneven. He can't walk a straight line. I don't think he knows where he's going."

"He must be delirious," said Hope. "Fever can do that."

The tracks were barely a yard from the brink when Captain changed course again. His nose to the ground, he crossed the road to the other side—the safe side. Hope felt a surge of relief.

The shadows were deepening. "I can't see his footprints any longer," said Elijah. "It's up to Captain to track him now."

The trail zigged and zagged away from the gorge and into the woods. Hope and Elijah followed, stumbling over the uneven ground. Suddenly Captain stopped, sniffed at something. Lying in the undergrowth was the wooden bucket. Hope picked it up. She felt inside. It was dry.

"Pa never made it to the well," she said.

"Then where did he go?" Elijah asked.

"Maybe he's wandering in the forest. I wish we had more light. If he's fallen, it will be hard to find him in the dark."

"Captain will find him . . . if he's in the forest," said Elijah. "I just hope he is in the forest and not . . ." Elijah glanced toward the gorge.

Hope, still carrying the bucket, pushed her way through a tangle of vines. Her foot caught on a tree root and she fell. Elijah hauled her to her feet.

"Are you hurt?"

"No. I'm fine. Don't worry about me." She picked up the bucket. Captain was waiting for them. He moved forward again, his nose to the ground as he led them this way and that until finally he left the woods and headed back toward the gorge.

Hope's heart filled with dread as the dog, his nose to the ground, moved closer and closer to the abyss. At the brink he stopped, looked back at them and whimpered. Elijah walked up to the edge. Numb with fear, Hope hung back. Setting down the bucket, she pressed her hands together and prayed. "Please, Lord. Spare my father. Don't take him now."

Pointing to a patch of raw earth where a small bush had been half pulled from the soil, Elijah said, "This is where he went over."

She edged closer to the brink, clutched Elijah's arm and looked own. A man lay motionless on a ledge twenty feet below. It was impossible to tell whether he was alive or dead.

"That's Pa." Hope felt as though a sliver of ice had entered her heart.

"If he's dead," Elijah said calmly, "it won't matter how long it takes to reach him. But if he's alive ..." No need to finish that sentence.

"How can we get to him?" Hope asked. The rocks were jagged and steep. She saw no way to climb down.

"There are no handholds." Elijah looked around. "I'll have to lower you to the ledge. I'll make a rope from grapevines. It will hold your weight."

"My weight? You plan to lower *me*?" Hope pulled back.

"You don't weigh more than a hundred pounds. I can handle that."

He probably can, she thought. *At least, I hope he can.* Her brother was strong and tall and outweighed her by fifty pounds. Since there was no possibility that she could lower him on a rope, he would have to lower her. There was no other way.

He had his tomahawk already pulled from his belt. Grapevines were everywhere, crawling up slopes and trailing from trees. The vines he chose had stems an inch or more thick, tough stems with ridged bark to give a good grip.

He handed her his knife. "You can strip off the leaves and fruit."

He chopped and she trimmed. Soon her hands were running with purple grape juice. After the vines were stripped, he spliced and twisted and bound them into a rope.

By the time their rope was made, only a few pink streaks still glowed in the western sky.

"Are you ready?" he asked.

"As ready as I'm ever likely to be." She kept her voice steady.

His eyes held hers in a hard, straight gaze. "When you reach the ledge, check to see if he's still alive. If he is, I'll throw down my blanket to keep him warm. Then you stay with him while I go to Butlersburg for help."

Hope took a deep breath. It was not the rope that she mistrusted, it was herself. She didn't think she could do it. She would faint with terror. She would lose her grip. She would miss the ledge and land on the scree of broken limestone hundreds of feet below. Or in the river. She wanted to tell him all this, but her tongue felt glued to the roof of her mouth.

Elijah took both her hands in his. She felt his warmth and strength flow into her. He said, "You are braver than you believe."

CHAPTER 34

Rescue

THE FIRST MOMENTS were the worst, until she found that her thighs, calves and ankles could help her to cling. The rough-barked stems were just the right thickness for a firm hold. She gripped with one hand while reaching down with the other to feel for the next good place to grab. The only sound she heard was the roaring in her ears. The only feeling she had was determination.

Hope barely breathed until she felt hard rock under her feet. "I've done it!" she gasped. Lowering herself to her hands and knees, she crouched over the unconscious man. She cupped his mouth with her hand and felt the warmth of his breath against her palm.

"He's alive!" she called to Elijah.

"Good. I'm going to pull up the rope to get it out of the way so the blanket won't catch on it. Then I'll throw a blanket to you. Cover him to keep him warm."

The rope of vines disappeared above her head. A minute later the blanket landed on the ledge. "I have it," she shouted.

"I'm leaving now," Elijah answered. "I'll go to Navy Hall. The duty officer can round up soldiers and rescue equipment. I'll guide them here. Don't expect us before morning. The men can't bring Pa up until there's enough light to see what they're doing."

Now the reality sank in. She would be here all night on this narrow ledge. Trying not to panic, Hope covered her father with the blanket and then sat down as far as from the edge as she could, pressing her back against the rock face.

Elijah's voice reached her again. "Captain will stay with you."

She didn't see how a dog on guard twenty feet over her head was going to give much protection. Yet she felt less alone just knowing he would be there.

Elijah spoke sharply to Captain. "Stay!"

A whimper.

"Good dog."

Silence. So Elijah had left. Someone at Navy Hall would be sure to recognize him. The deserter. Yet he had not hesitated to go there any more than she had hesitated to descend the cliff. "We're birds of a feather," she said to herself, "my brother and I."

Her hands hurt where the vines' rough bark had scraped her skin. The roaring in her ears stopped. Now she heard all sorts of sounds. The wind. The river. The jarring of night-hawks as they swooped over the gorge, scooping up their evening meal of mosquitoes and other flying insects. There were bats, too, but they made no noise. Bats usually made her nervous, but not tonight. They were living creatures, like her.

There was one good thing about the dark. It kept her from seeing how far down she still might fall. Not that she wished to look. She remembered the way the bottom of the gorge had seemed to lift toward her, and how she had wanted to jump.

The stars came out, first the bright one that she knew was not really a star. It was a planet. But people called it the Evening Star. Then the moon rose, full and bright. Its colour was orange tonight. Why was that?

The moon gave off enough light for her to see her father's face. He looked old. He was old. A sick old man. A feeling of tenderness spread through her, and she reached under the blanket to take his hand.

His hand was icy cold. Gradually she felt it warm within her grasp. He opened his eyes, looked into her eyes. "Pa," she said, "it's me. Hope." He closed his eyes again. She held his hand all night.

Toward dawn the wind died down. Now the only sound was the rushing water below. The bats flew away. The moon set. Sitting on the ledge, holding her father's limp hand, she watched the eastern sky fade from black to grey. As the first rays of the rising sun appeared over the top of the opposite riverbank, she heard an eerie racket that grew louder and louder. A flock of wild geese was flying up the gorge, honking as they soared. They passed in front of her, at least fifty geese so close that she heard the flapping of their great wings. Above her head, Captain barked.

The geese had scarcely disappeared from sight when she heard male voices overhead. One of them was her brother's voice. Hope looked up. Elijah and half-a-dozen soldiers wearing forage caps were peering over the brink.

The rescue was conducted in an orderly way. First, a knotted rope was slung over the rim of the gorge, and then a soldier climbed down the rope, carrying a harness. He thrust Hope into it, awkwardly pushing and pulling her limbs to fit a strap between her legs and another under her arms and around her chest.

"On your way up," he said, "use your hands to push away from the rock face so you won't bump." These were the only words he uttered before calling, "Heave, ho!" to the men above. Up she went, hoisted into the air. Moments later, she was lying on the dry, skimpy grass at the top.

The soldiers freed her from the harness. "Thank you," she mumbled as she unsteadily rose to her feet. The soldiers carried the harness back to the brink and lowered it to the soldier waiting on the ledge. Elijah lined up with the others to hold the rope. She watched them brace themselves as if this were a tug-of-war. After a few minutes they hauled her father to the top.

Now suddenly, when she saw that he was safe, the strength ran out of her. She heard the soldiers talking earnestly, but their voices were a blur of sound. Everything around her turned grey, then black, and the ground rose up and hit her on the head.

She had no sense of time passing. When she regained consciousness, Elijah was holding her hand.

"You fainted."

"I've never done that before."

"It's all right. I think you're the bravest girl I've ever known, and there are some mighty brave Cherokee girls." He sat her up. "Now let's see what shape you're in. How do you feel?"

"I'm fine."

He placed his hand on the back of her head. "You have a bit of a bump. Except for a few scrapes, there's no other damage that I can see."

She turned her head toward the brink. The soldiers had placed her father on a stretcher. She watched as they carried him into the cabin. Elijah pulled Hope to her feet, and they followed.

The soldiers laid the old man on his bed. Without a word, they left Hope and Elijah with him. She stepped close to Elijah. He put his arm around her. She had not noticed Captain, but now she saw that he was with them, too.

"Pa's in bad shape," said Elijah.

There was a bloody rip in one leg of his filthy breeches, and under the rip a gash that oozed blood. His eyes were closed but his mouth was open, a black hole. At the sight of him, Hope knew that she was about to burst into tears, but she also knew that this was something she must not do.

"How can we help him?" she asked.

"There's little we can do."

Hope felt her throat close up. She nodded but could not speak. One month ago, her father had looked merely sick. Now he appeared close to death. Under the sheen of sweat, his skin was greenish grey. His bushy eyebrows jutted sharply above the sunken hollows of his eyes. The lids were shut. His breath wheezed. He did not move except when a wince of pain went through him.

Elijah pulled her gently to the door. "Let him rest."

When they left the cabin, they found the six soldiers standing at ease. The one who appeared to be in charge stepped forward.

"Private Cobman, you are under arrest."

"Yes," Elijah said calmly, "I suppose I am."

Hope waited for the soldiers to snap manacles on him, but nothing happened. They didn't look as if they wanted to arrest him. Elijah looked from one to another. After a long silence, he said to the soldier in charge. "Sergeant, if I give my word that I won't try to escape, will you allow me to stay with my father? You can see that it won't be for very long."

"I have no authority to let you remain at liberty solely on the basis of your promise not to run away," the sergeant replied. "You might mean it now, but a few hours consideration could easily change your mind."

"I understand." Elijah held out his hands for the manacles.

"My orders are to return the platoon to Navy Hall. I should take you with us." The sergeant cleared his throat. "It took a lot of courage for you to walk right into Navy Hall last night. You knew you'd be up for a court martial. That's didn't stop you. Private Cobman, you are a brave man."

"John Cobman is my father. I couldn't have done anything else."

The sergeant cleared his throat again. "I'm going to let you stay."

He picked two men to remain behind as guards. Elijah's reprieve would last for twenty-four hours. Then the platoon would return. If for any reason Elijah left the cabin, the guards were not to let him out of their sight.

The guards went with him to pick up the water bucket from the edge of the gorge and fill it with fresh water from the neighbour's well.

CHAPTER 35

I Bequeath

ELIJAH CUT AWAY THE fabric of his father's breeches, washed the wound and applied an ointment that he carried in his pouch. Then he and Hope sat down, she on one side of the bed, and Elijah on the other. For hours they watched their father's chest move up and down while listening to the rattle in his chest. Hope was beginning to think that he would never wake up, that sometime that day or during the night, he would pass away without opening his eyes. He would depart peacefully from this world to whatever lay beyond.

Late in the afternoon a strong wind rose. It whistled and moaned through the chinks and cracks in the window frames, under the door and between the logs. A draft blew down the chimney, making the fire sputter and filling the cabin with stinging, eye-watering smoke.

She was wiping her eyes when her father woke. He did not speak for a few moments but watched her steadily. Finally he said, "So you're really here."

"Yes, I'm here."

"I thought it must be a dream."

"No dream. Elijah's here, too." She wanted to say more, but a sore lump seemed to have lodged in her throat.

"Elijah is here?"

"Both of us," said Elijah.

Pa turned his head. His eyes lit up when he saw his son. "I never expected to see you again."

"I had to come. There are things I need to tell you."

"Then do it now. You won't have another chance." He gave a terrible cough.

Hope rose, took a cup from the shelf and dipped it into the water bucket. She raised her father's shoulders and held the cup to his lips while he drank.

"Thank you, Hope," he said, then spoke again to Elijah. "Say what you've come to say."

"I'll get right to the point," said Elijah. "I came here to tell you that Hope is as much your child as I am. Hope says you don't believe it."

Pa turned his head to look at Hope. "I can see that you believe it, dear young lady. You proved that last night. No daughter could show more devotion. I receive it with great gratitude. I'd be proud to be your father, but . . ." He coughed. Blood dribbled from the corner of his mouth.

"Not good enough," said Elijah. He rose from his chair, walked around the bed to stand at Hope's side and looked down at his father. "I was thirteen when you and Silas left. There are things a woman can't easily talk about to a boy that age. But Ma was already with child when you left. She didn't know it, or at least she wasn't sure. A few months later, when her condition was clear, she explained to me that she'd thought at first it was just her age affecting her. That made sense. She had a son twenty years old. She thought she was too old to conceive." Elijah stopped for breath, and then continued. "I swear to you that there was no other man anywhere about. I can't fathom how you could imagine such a thing, knowing Ma. Church every Sunday. Grace before meals. No swearing. Not one drop of spirits in the house. No woman could be stricter in her morals. And I can tell you one more thing. Every day, she was on her knees praying for your safe return."

"Enough!" Pa raised his hand. "Stop! You need say no more. You make me ashamed. Completely ashamed." His hand fell back down onto his blanket. "What can I do to make amends?"

"Acknowledge Hope as your daughter, and do it in a way that the world will recognize. Make your will. Name her as your heir."

"Not just her. You too."

"That doesn't matter."

"It matters to me. Get me paper and a pen."

"Where will I find them?" Elijah asked.

"On the shelf by the door."

Elijah looked around. He saw the rough shelf that was supported by pegs driven between the logs. On it were a Bible, a stack of paper, an ink pot and a quill. When Elijah had fetched the writing materials, Hope raised her father's shoulders and held him so that he rested against her chest. She had been through this before. First her mother, now her father. It was hard, bitter grief to lose them both.

Elijah brought the Bible to provide a hard surface for writing. He spread the sheet of paper on the Bible, dipped the quill into the ink pot and placed it in his father's hand.

The old man mouthed the words as he wrote:

"In the name of God, Amen. I, John George Cobman, of West Niagara, Concerning the uncertainty of this Mortal life . . ."

The quill needed ink. Elijah, holding the ink pot, dipped the quill and gave it back to his father.

". . . and being of Sound Mind and Memory, thanks be to Almighty God for the same . . ."

More ink required.

". . . do make this my last Will and Testament in manner and form following . . ."

Again, more ink.

Merciful Heavens! Were all these words necessary? Hope could see that her father looked tired, that his hand was shaking and the writing uneven. Would he have the strength to finish? Elijah's eyes met hers. Was he wondering the same thing?

"Pa," said Elijah, "would you like me to write all this down? Then you can read it over before you sign it."

"No, these are my own words, and they must be written by my own hand. I'm nearly there." Elijah dipped the quill for him again.

"That is to say, I give and bequeath my land and all other worldly goods to my son Elijah and my daughter Hope, to be divided equally between them."

He looked over what he had written. The letters were misshapen and the lines uneven, but legible. "We'll need a witness to my signature," he said.

"There are two men who can witness it waiting outside." Elijah motioned to Hope that she should call them. In moments they were there.

"Do you know the date?" the old man asked.

"October 1, 1791," one soldier answered.

Pa signed his name and wrote the date. "I have done," he said. Taking the pen from his father's hand, Elijah let out his breath in an enormous sigh of relief. The soldiers signed as witnesses and left the cabin.

Pa lay back down again. Making his will had left him exhausted. After a minute he tried to rise, fell back. Hope thought he would not speak again. But he was not finished.

"Hope," he said. "Daughter." He gave a weak smile. "Daughter," he repeated, as if he liked the sound of the word. "Please forgive me."

"Nothing to forgive."

"Is there anything you can ask of me that I can grant?"

Hope hesitated. There was one question that had troubled her for a long time. It seemed unkind to ask it at such a time. But her father wanted to make amends, and if she did not ask, she would wonder for the rest of her life.

"Pa, if you could tell me why you never tried to find Ma."

"Ah, that's a question with which I've often reproached myself." He paused. "At first there was no way to look for her. I didn't know whether she was still in Canajoharie, because so many Loyalists had fled. Colonel Butler kept the Rangers together. He was arranging to settle his regiment on land bought from the Mississaugas. Then it took three years for the land to be surveyed. So I waited. I told myself I'd look for Sadie as soon as I got my location ticket and built a cabin. Until then, I had no home to bring her to." He stopped speaking, coughed weakly.

"More water?" Hope asked.

He nodded. After sipping a little, he continued, "The work went slowly. By the time I had land cleared and the cabin built, the sickness was taking hold of me. I knew what was coming. I'd seen people die from consumption. How could I take care of a wife? She'd just be taking care of me. And anyway, by that time I lacked the strength to start looking. I expected to die alone." He looked at Hope and Elijah, both standing at his bedside. "Having you here seems a miracle to me."

He closed his eyes and a look of peace came over his face. Hope waited, thinking more remained to be said. A blessing, at least. She prayed that he would rally again, but that was all. The hours passed. Just before sunset, his breathing stopped.

"He's gone," said Elijah.

"Goodbye, Pa," Hope said. She walked away and stood in a corner of the cabin. She did not try to stop her tears. Her knees gave way. She sat on the floor. Sobs shook her whole body.

She felt Elijah's hands on her shoulders, and she heard his voice. "Come with me. Come outside." He helped her to her feet, and she leaned against him while they left the cabin. The soldiers were standing together. When they saw Hope and Elijah come out, they took off their forage caps.

CHAPTER 36

Honourable Discharge

"WHAT SHALL WE DO NOW?" Hope asked.

"Dig a grave," said Elijah. "There's a spade leaning against the side of the cabin. I'll make a start before it gets too dark."

"While you do that, I can look for something to eat. Those soldiers must be hungry, too." She went inside. It seemed wrong to think about food with Pa's body lying there. But those who live must eat. She approached the bed and folded her father's hands upon his chest and then pulled up a blanket to cover his face. "Rest in peace," she said softly.

Hope turned to the shelf that held the cabin's meagre supply of food. She found rice, salt pork, tea and dry biscuits. It wouldn't be much of a meal, but it would do.

As she got supper ready, she checked twice to see how the digging was coming along. There must have been two spades, because one of the soldiers was helping Elijah to dig. The other sat with his musket across his knees, watching.

She carried the food outside. They ate silently, quickly. Then the digging resumed. When it was too dark to dig, Elijah came into the cabin. The two soldiers settled down to guard duty outside the door.

Elijah remained slumped on the chair, his head bowed. Hope sat on the stool, watching him. She did not think that he would sleep tonight, knowing that in the morning he would be taken away to face a court martial. If the court sentenced him to face a firing squad, he would pay a high price for saving the life of a man who was soon to die anyway. It was so unfair! Elijah would lose his life. She would lose her brother. Hundreds of miles away, a Cherokee woman named Swims Deep would lose her husband, and a child would grow up fatherless. Hope knew what that was like.

What would happen, she wondered, if Elijah tried to escape? The idea tempted her. She imagined flinging open the door, Elijah vaulting over the two drowsy guards and vanishing into the night.

But he would not do such a thing, and she wasn't sure she would want him to. The death of Sergeant Malcolm had cost him too much. He had told her that he would rather die than take the life of another. By escaping, he might do the very thing he had sworn never to do, for if Elijah ran off, the sergeant who had taken a chance by letting him stay at his dying father's bedside might himself meet death against the wall.

Elijah stirred, muttered something indistinguishable.

"Elijah?" she said.

"What?"

"When the platoon comes back, do you suppose the soldiers will wait till after we have a proper burial? I mean, at least say some prayers before they take you away?"

"Probably. Pa was a soldier. They'll want to show respect."

"At Ma's funeral, the Reverend Mr. Stuart read a Bible lesson. It began, 'I am the resurrection and the life.'"

"I know the passage," said Elijah. "I can find it in Pa's Bible. Now why don't you take your blanket, lie down on the floor and get some sleep?"

"I won't be able to sleep."

"Try it."

She tried it, and she did.

At dawn Elijah and the soldiers finished digging the grave. Hope and Elijah wrapped their father in one of his musty blankets as a winding sheet. At the graveside, Elijah read the Bible passage. All four said the Lord's Prayer. One of the soldiers recited the Psalm that began, "The Lord is my shepherd."

Hope thought they handled the burial very well. After it was over, Hope, Elijah and the soldiers sat down on the grass outside the cabin and ate what was left of the rice and pork she had boiled up the evening before. Now there was nothing to do but wait for the platoon to return to take Elijah away. Already the morning was half gone.

The platoon did not return. Instead, it was Ensign Godfrey Dunn who joined them. He was carrying a leather document case.

"Colonel Butler has sent me as his emissary," Godfrey said, "to deliver a document of interest to Private Cobman."

Dressed in his full regimentals, Godfrey was certainly attired for an important occasion. His scarlet coat was freshly pressed and his cross bands were pipeclayed to snowy whiteness. On his head was his tall shako hat. Godfrey took off his hat respectfully at the grave and stood for a moment with his head bowed. After he had done that, he opened the document case, pulled out a paper and gave it to Elijah

As Elijah read, his eyes opened wide. The paper shook in his hand. When he had finished, he said, "I can't believe it."

Hope looked from Elijah's astonished face to Godfrey's happy grin. "What does it say?" she demanded. "Read it aloud!"

Elijah took a deep breath:

> *To all whom it may concern.*
>
> *These are to Certify that the Bearer hereof Elijah Cobman Private Soldier has served honestly and faithfully in The King's Royal Regiment of New York and thereafter under the Command of Major Patrick Ferguson in his Special Corps a total of thirteen years,*

but from a long series of Hardships undergone in the Carolinas being Rendered infirm & incapable of further Service is hereby Discharged.

Given under my hand & seal at Niagara the 2nd day of October in the year 1791

John Butler, Colonel

Commander in Chief, the Nassau & Lincoln Militia.

Elijah looked up. "No court martial. No . . ." His voice trailed away. He looked stunned.

"You're free to go or to stay," said Godfrey, "as you like."

CHAPTER 37

Ska-noh

HOPE AND ELIJAH SPENT the night in the cabin. The next morning Elijah packed his gear. Hope urged him to take anything he wanted. "It's half yours," she insisted. "It isn't fair for me to have it all."

"There's nothing I want." He picked up Pa's rifle, inspected it, sighted along the barrel. Then he gave a little shake to his head and set it down. "I don't believe I'll ever fire a gun again. But you should learn to use it. Living here alone, you must be able to protect yourself."

"I have Captain."

"He'll be a first-rate guard dog when he finishes growing up, but even then . . ."

"You're right. I'll learn to shoot. I'm sure I can find some-one to teach me."

"Someone?" he laughed. "I'm certain that Ensign Dunn will be only too glad to instruct you." Elijah slung his carry-ing basket onto his back and his quiver over his shoulder. He picked up the bow. "I'll be off. I can't lose more time if I'm to be in Chickamauga before Freezing Moon."

She stood for a moment with him outside the door. It was a brilliant fall day, the forest aflame with colour. A blue jay screeched as it took flight from a scarlet maple tree.

Elijah gave Hope a hug and then stepped back, still hold-ing her hands. "*Ska-noh*," he said. "It means 'Be strong.' That's one of my few Mohawk words. Okwaho said it when we parted many years ago. I thought we'd never meet again. But we did." He paused. "Same with you and me, Sister, though I won't try to predict how or where or when."

"*Ska-noh*." She tried to smile. "You don't need to worry about me. I can look after myself."

"I know you can."

Hope followed him with her eyes as he walked up the path from the cabin to the road. When he turned south and she could no longer see him, she went inside with Captain.

Standing beside the closed door, she looked around at all the furnishings and other things that now belonged to her: bed, table, chairs, blankets, pots and pans. She looked further and found a hammer, a saw and a wash tub. *So this is to be my home*, she thought. *I may as well make a start*. She picked up the wooden bucket that stood under the shelf. To fill the washtub would require three trips to the neighbour's well.

The next day she strung up a clothes line and was hanging a thoroughly scrubbed blanket to dry when Godfrey arrived to ask how she was managing. He also brought an invitation to tea from Mrs. Hill, the kind woman who had given her a room for the night after her father turned her away. Godfrey was included in the invitation, he told her, and would be pleased to escort her there.

As Elijah had suggested, she asked Godfrey whether he would be able to instruct her on the care and use of a rifle. He would be delighted, he assured her. Her first lesson took place that very day. Godfrey found it necessary to put his arm around her shoulders while teaching her to hold the rifle. His cheek pressed hers while she learned to aim. She found the experience delightfully warming. When he suggested that many more lessons were required, she agreed.

The following week Godfrey helped her to write a letter to Charlotte, advising Hope on spelling while insisting that the pen be in her hand. In her letter, Hope told Charlotte about her long journey with Elijah, and she asked if Charlotte could arrange for her trunk to be shipped on the packet boat from Milltown to Niagara, for the trunk was still at Charlotte's home. Hope thought wistfully about the blue gown with white dots that she had bought from Mary during her stay at Mrs. Fairley's sewing establishment. She certainly would like Godfrey to see her wearing that pretty gown!

A month passed. On a blustery November day Hope sat on her chair and watched fat drip into the flames from the goose roasting on the spit. The goose was a gift from Godfrey, who had shot a dozen of them during the fall migration. Hope kept a dipperful of water handy in case the goose caught fire, which had been the fate of the last one he gave her.

From time to time she rose from her chair, turned the crank to rotate the spit, and then sat down again. Rain beat on the roof and a strong north wind rattled the little panes of window glass. A month ago, such a wind would have blown down through the chimney, throwing sparks from the fire, scattering ash and filling the cabin with smoke.

It had cost Hope one pound to have the chimney fixed. She had hired a mason to climb onto the roof to make the chimney taller by adding two courses of stone. She had also paid a carpenter to replace the glass in the broken window. The price for that had been four shillings. Now her cabin was snug and warm, although after these expenditures little was left of the three pounds Ephraim had paid as her wages.

There were other improvements that she had achieved at no cost and with no one's help. She had gathered moss with which she stuffed the chinks between the logs and around the window frames. She had cleaned the cabin, washing everything with soap that she made by boiling fat with white ashes from the fire.

While scrubbing the floor, she had found a tea tin stuffed with money under one of the planks. There were paper bank notes and silver coins. Pa had not mentioned this treasure trove. In his sickness he must have forgotten about it. She counted the money carefully, because half belonged to Elijah and someday, somehow, she would give it to him. Her own share amounted to three pounds, four shillings. Some of that windfall paid for a new well, the site carefully chosen to avoid seepage from the resting place of the dead raccoon.

This was the month of her birthday fourteen years ago. "Freezing Moon" was what the native people called it. Far away in Chickamauga, Elijah and Swims Deep's baby would soon be born, perhaps had already been born. *I'm going to be an aunt*, she thought, *to a Cherokee child*. That was an interesting and pleasing idea. Hope was happy to think that her brother was getting on with his life, as she was with hers.

She spent days thinking about what to do with the rest of her part of the money hidden under the floor. Upon making a decision, she shared her thoughts with Captain, who lay on the floor next to her chair, enjoying the warmth of the fire.

"I have enough money," she explained to the dog, "to hire a carpenter to build a shed with nesting boxes and to buy a couple of dozen chickens." She paused and spoke very clearly. "Chickens, Captain. You can help me take care of them."

Captain raised his head, cocked his ears and looked at her. His eyes were bright with interest.

"I can sell the eggs to the garrison. If all goes well, I'll buy a cow in the spring. Then we'll have milk and butter as well as eggs. I can plant a vegetable garden. But chickens come first.

I won't give them names." She paused, thinking how she'd learned that lesson the hard way.

She gave Captain's head a pat. "We've come a long way together since the day I fetched you from the Andersons' farm. You were so little I had to carry you part of the way." Captain's tail gave a thump on the floor. "Adam made the right choice," Hope continued, "when he picked you to be my dog."

Hope was rubbing Captain's thick, wiry coat, but she was thinking about Adam. Although she had escaped the drudgery of working for the Blocks, he was still trapped by the duty he owed to his family. "I'll be old and grey," he had complained, "by the time I get to go anywhere." Poor Adam. His life had seemed so bleak to him the last time she saw him. But he was a boy with spunk and confidence, not the kind who would give up easily. In a couple of years his younger brothers, the twins, would be old enough to give their father the help he needed to carve a farm from the wilderness. Then Adam would be on his way. He would not have to wait until he was old and grey to follow his dream.

Captain laid his muzzle on his forepaws and went to sleep. While Hope gazed at the leaping flames, her thoughts turned next to Elijah. Someday, maybe when she least expected it, a message would arrive from him. Or maybe she would look up to see him coming along the path toward her, his bow over his shoulder, walking with an easy stride. In the meantime, she had plenty to do to fill her life.

She still had one more brother to find, she reminded herself. Moses, called Broken Trail. Someday she would find him, too. She felt quite sure of this. For a girl named Hope, all things were possible.

ACKNOWLEDGEMENTS

I give my warm thanks to the generous and knowledgeable people who found time to help me with this novel. The list begins with Donald Combe, Archivist of St. Mark's Church, Niagara-on-the-Lake. I only wish I could also thank Mrs. Elizabeth Simcoe (1766–1850), wife of the first lieutenant-governor, because her diary more than any other single source brought to life for me the early days of Upper Canada. I should also like to thank the staff at the Niagara Historical Society Museum, who patiently answered my questions and brought to my attention *The Capital Years: Niagara-on-the-Lake 1792–1796*, a book which is a treasure trove of specific information.

Looking across the border, I acknowledge with gratitude the helpfulness of the guides at Old Fort Niagara, Youngstown, New York, who shared with me their knowledge of that fort's history all the way back to 1678.

My special thanks are reserved for those who have supported my writing the longest: my daughter Alison Baxter Lean, who invariably accepts with grace the unenviable task of critiquing my first drafts; and my writing friends Barbara Ledger, Debbie Welland, Susan Evans Shaw, Alexandra Gall and Linda Helson of the Canadian Federation of University Women, Hamilton Branch.

This book is immeasurably stronger for the editorial attention it received at Ronsdale Press. I would especially like to thank Ronald and Veronica Hatch for their insightful criticism, which helped me to see new possibilities in the story I had set out to tell.

ABOUT THE AUTHOR

Although Jean Rae Baxter was born in Toronto and grew up in Hamilton, "down home" was the region of Essex and Kent Counties on the shores of Lake Erie where her ancestors had settled, some following the American Revolution and some a century earlier, in the days of New France. There were many family stories to awaken her interest in Canada's past.

After graduating from the University of Toronto and Queen's University, she became a secondary school teacher in Lennox & Addington County, a part of Ontario particularly rich in United Empire Loyalist history. It was during her career as a teacher that she saw the need for historical fiction written from a Canadian point of view, for at that time almost everything in books, television and movies had an American bias.

It was to provide a Canadian alternative view that she wrote *The*

Way Lies North (2007). In this novel she focused upon the plight of ordinary white Loyalists driven from their homes by the violence of the American Revolution. This book was followed by *Broken Trail* (2011), which told of the native people's struggle. The third novel, *Freedom Bound* (2012), dealt with the Black Loyalists. In *The White Oneida* (2014), Baxter examined the issues facing the native people following the American War of Independence as they strove to form a confederacy of their own.

Hope's Journey, the fifth book in what has now become known as the "Forging a Nation Series," is set in 1791. It shows the determination of Loyalist refugees to build not just new lives but a new country in the aftermath of war.

In addition to reading and writing, Jean loves travel, gardening and dogs. She visits many schools and libraries to talk about Canadian history and to conduct creative writing workshops, particularly enjoying those for "Teens and Tweens." You will learn more about her writing on her website, www.jeanraebaxter.ca. You may contact her at jeanraebaxter@sympatico.ca or visit her on Facebook at www.facebook.com/JeanRaeBaxterBooks.